HAROLD

HAROLD
by
Miles Wylie

Yes, in the tavern I too have been seated.
For me, as for the rest, the wine was meted
Goethe

Applecourt Books

Kings Lynn

Harold

© Miles Wylie 2023

978-1-9168846-7-0

First Edition
Applecourt Books
Kings Lynn

camerajournal@hotmail.com

Typeset and designed by Paul Sutton

For E.

Mały dowód niemałej przyjaźni

CHAPTER I

Fred, looking not very much worse than usual, descended the staircase leading from domestic quarters where, it was said, arguments raged on a nightly basis with a wife never put on view. He took his place behind the pumps.

'Ah,' Colin said, 'the merry landlord.'

'Morning, gents.'

'A thick night, Frederick?'

'You could say that, Mr Bailey.'

'Two pints of your finest ale, if you would be so kind.'

Indisposed to further conversation and, I now saw, sporting the beginnings of a black eye, Fred pulled the beer. We took our tankards over to a table and sat down.

'Fred has trouble with the lady of his bosom,' Bailey said. 'Do you have a lady of your bosom who gives you trouble?' He gave one of his twitches when he said that, as if he were responding to an account of an entanglement of my own, foreseen to be explosive enough in quality to prompt a physical reaction. Even in a more congenial setting than the drab public house where the Academy meeting had been convened, Colin Bailey was not the person to whom to confide my present emotional standing, however long or short a prospectus he was offered on the ways of love. All Bailey would have to say after it, would be 'Jolly good'. Then he would change the subject.

' "Now heaven be thanked I am out of love." '

'Johnny Keats?'

'Jan Struther. Her real name was Joyce Anstruther. She's remembered now only for a novel, *Mrs Miniver*. It was made into a film. Ages before our day.'

'Oh, jolly good.'

Bailey looked around him. He was not bookish. Far from it. It could be said unkindly that it was surprising he had even heard of Keats. He held his beer glass up to the light as if he expected to locate a small creature swimming in its depths and turned to a newspaper he retrieved from his jacket pocket. I fell to wondering whether love, which I had denied myself, as opposed to failing to re-ignite ever since Ann's death, had been an especially rewarding eventuality. My feeling was that I had been a bit of an ass to have been carried along by an emo-

7

tion so easily susceptible to being smashed in pieces. Love is by its very nature short-lived, reliance upon the beloved for its maintenance at the requisite pitch never to be absolutely relied upon. On recovering from my sorrow, the construction of a shield against love and its minor derivatives – tenderness, sociability, fellow-feeling – had been surprisingly easy to forge. Even for Ganson, who had been kindness itself in shepherding me through my grief considering he was himself burdened with the loss of his own wife in the same car accident, I felt little affection, a coolness extending as well to my son George and to Ann's parents who were bringing him up.

I was contentedly melancholic (not of course happily so) but then melancholia is by no means an unpleasant state of mind although it is to some extent reliant for its upkeep on its owner's being reasonably well-off, in the same way that hunger and thirst are far from unpleasant sensations provided one knows that there is meat and drink available round the corner. I had got it into my head, rightly or wrongly, that a modest financial stability sustaining this mental outlook ought not to be revealed to the man kind enough to have offered employment in his Academy to someone who for a while had been, as my mother-in-law phrased it, 'put away.' In my spare time, of which there was plenty, I worked on an historical account of the village where I lived. I ate meals in the ground-floor café below my flat and drank in the town pub nearest the Academy where my only friends – that is to say, associates – were Ganson and his teaching staff.

One night soon after my 'release' to use my psychiatrist's word, Ganson and I had been drinking in the Jolly Herring for some while, 'giving it a bit of a nudge,' in Bailey's phrase. It was Ganson's theory, a summary there seemed no purpose in disputing, that Dr du Sautoy or his drugs, a mixture of both he thought, had instilled in me a life-pattern somewhere between lassitude and *laissez-faire*: impassivity not altogether too harsh a word. I was like the jolly miller in the song, Ganson summed up: 'I care for nobody, no not I, if nobody cares for me.'

Analysis of the words continued, illustrated by Ganson with snatches from the song loudly carolled out. I remarked that unlike the jolly miller I did not sing from morn to night nor was I as blithe as a lark. 'Granted, granted. But you work from morn to night in my English department and still speaking in granular terms you do not fear next quarter-day, although heaven knows how you send George to a private school on the money I pay you.'

'And I merrily push the can about…'

'And drink and sing with glee,' Ganson concluded, rising up and hollering out the song's last words. Fred called for less noise.

Recently when teaching an English poetry class – Ganson had rather I said 'hosting a seminar' – on the theme of melancholy – here again Ganson preferred 'depression' – I had suggested that vexation of the spirits had its good points. It had been gratifying to have been told by a student that I had enabled her to accept the gloom she had been taking for a malady as representing no more than a part of her natural constitution.

Colin Bailey took a pull at his glass of beer. 'Drink up, Lay-o-nar,' he said, pronouncing my name as if it were French. 'We must empty these beakers before the Dean arrives. Remind me, what is the purpose behind today's foregathering? It has slipped what I am amused to call my mind. I am given to understand we are to expect a full house.'

'We are here to discuss Project SWOT, Sunk Without Trace, the Dean's latest brainwave which, I am ashamed to say, I put into his head. The idea can be categorised as yet another of his "shots in the arm".'

Bailey bowed his head in forgiveness of a serious lapse of discretion. In point of fact I did not know why Ganson had required his presence at this particular meeting. This prompted a query of my own: 'What are you doing here, Colin?'

I asked the question only because the professors of the small college of further education where I taught had been convened by our Dean on a purely academic matter. Bailey was our bursar, offering no pretence to scholarship, if that was the word applicable to our faculty, except for a head for figures. Perhaps not even that. He was nicknamed Backstairs Bailey – shortened to 'Stairs' – because of an ability to manage the financial side of the Academy efficiently and equally, or so it was thought, to his own advantage. His past was said to have been of a combative nature, spent flying aircraft, the names of which were sometimes dropped into conversation – Typhoon, Lockheed, Tornado – in daredevil aerobatics. Stephen Aldhouse, Fine Arts, had dismissed this background as a lot of old madam, using an expression of Bailey's to point up statements that were open to question, at the same time offering a less intrepid account of Bailey's flying days if any there had been. 'I'll bet he was the one with the long hair and suede shoes in the centrally heated control room who sticks different coloured pins into maps to show people the areas that are to be targeted: "Be careful of the mauve ones, boys, they're ever so sharp." Aldhouse performed a shockingly effeminate, and, as far as was known, unwarranted, imitation of Bailey at the map board. 'Not of course that there was a war when Stairs was in the armed forces: if indeed he ever was.'

It could be that Bailey had not been ordered to attend, that he had turned up merely in expectation of the free round of drinks, more than one if the meeting overran its time, that he was confident Ganson would provide. He interpreted my question as one that demanded an infinitely wider, a far more teasingly philosophical, response than he felt up to offering after only one pint of beer.

'What are any of us doing here, old boy?'

He lapsed into silent contemplation of his personal destiny: mine too perhaps in the light of my confession of having made trouble within the Academy's ranks.

On the morning when the whole business began, Ganson and I had been out for a stroll, talking of nothing in particular. For some time we hadn't met anybody. That was cause for thanksgiving. Ganson would often bend over dogs on leads in the way Swinburne is said to have kissed babies in prams, at the same time voicing to their owners his preference for cats, leading to a debate that could hamper progress to wherever we were headed. Today a dog-owner had passed unmolested. A young girl with holes in the knees of her jeans was given but a glancing look and allowed to go on her way. Ganson had been to known to stop women dressed in these fashionably tattered clothes and submit them to a searching enquiry as to the morality of masquerading as a person of such acute poverty that she was forced to walk the streets in rags. A big car had passed us, a chauffeur at the wheel. My son had identified the model as a Flying Spur. As a general rule any vehicle considered by Ganson to be over-ornate became a target for his gunnery. He would snap to attention and present a military salute to the driver as he went by, immediately afterwards thumbing his nose and sticking out his tongue at the tail-lights of the car after it had driven past. Today he looked at it admiringly: 'That's a handsome beast.' I recognized the driver as Drake, an Academy student with whom I occasionally had breakfast in my downstairs café.

At that point my mobile telephone had rung. In the normal course of events, nothing could have been more likely to get up Ganson's nose. 'There's nobody at the other end, you know,' he would loudly remark to his companion as the caller passed by. 'It's just a toy they bought at Hamley's, two ninety-nine, batteries not included.' On other occasions, Ganson might content himself with a smiling comment: 'Does he (or she) still love you?' was a standard Ganson interrogation.

The call could only be from George. Nobody else knew the number. A voice, not George's, although of equally treble pitch, asked to speak to Felix. I replied in German.

'*Einen Moment, bitte.*'

I felt for the crib George had instructed me always to carry in my breast pocket in case of this sort of emergency. I looked up Felix on the list and changed intonation.

'Felix speakin'. Yeah. Tell your mate to concentrate real hard. I'm art-o'-doors and foughts are difficult to pick up art-o'-doors.' I counted to ten and then said, 'The card what you're lookin' at is the free of diamonds.' I resumed the German voice. 'Felix now must finish. These experiments are for him so tiring.' I rang off.

'What the hell are you playing at?'

'Collaborating with George on a conjuring trick. I can reveal no more than that. George is insistent on secrecy in all things magical. Suffice it to say that if the caller had asked to speak to Henry and not to Felix the correct card would have been – '. I glanced at my crib – 'the ten of clubs.'

'You were a bit of a conjuror at school, I recall.'

'Not as good as you. I still don't know how you did that ectoplasm bit.'

'*Nom d'une pipe*, don't bring that up again. And I'd prefer you not to talk to the others about those spook experiments of ours. Especially to Scott McLeod. In a profession like ours, one likes to be thought of as having one's feet firmly on the ground.'

Ganson had a point. We all have one secret, not necessarily a dark one, one nonetheless better kept to ourselves. I could claim to a secret of my own, two secrets in fact, or, as it turned out, the one a sub-division of the other. Ganson's interest in the mystical affairs we pursued when we had been at school together may have attuned him later on to the possibility of intelligent life on other planets. This had resulted in an unlooked-for and disastrous change in his professional career.

He had founded AHEAD (Academy for Higher Education) after his dismissal from Cambridge. It was never made absolutely clear how this disgrace came about. I had heard the story from several sources, each one contributing a small section to a canvas too unfinished to present a clear picture of events. Three or so years after we had abandoned our occult exploits Ganson, still at school, aged about sixteen, had edited an alternative magazine, more or less a *samizdat*, to be circulated on Speech Day along with the official school journal. He called it *Droppings*. It had featured his first exercise in textual scholarship, an article entitled 'Some Insufficiencies in the GCSE edition of *Volpone*'. This had been picked up by a Cambridge professor who got it reprinted in an issue of an academic quarterly, bringing Ganson's precocious scholarship to the notice of literary bigwigs. He then went up to university where he had risen rapidly as an expert in his chosen field of research and had been given the job of founding a new department specialising in bibliographical studies.

A young American student who was at work on Melville – possibly Hawthorne – had caught Ganson's eye. In the course of her tuition periods, probably also on some extramural evenings out, she let it be known of her affiliation to a select body of young people back home who had made contact with the more influential inhabitants of the planet Mercury. These men were priests, revered by all other Mercurians of both sexes – if sexes they possessed – who encouraged their earthly communicants, again of both sexes, to get on better terms with the planet by spreading the word of their existence to those thought worthy of the secret. These hierophants, who were to be estimated as more broadminded than the established priesthood here on earth, had nothing against the relationship between a tutor and a younger votary in his care. They had other things on their mind.

To put it bluntly, they were after money. Here was where Ganson's enthusiasm for this intergalactic joining of hands was put to the test. The student who had whispered to him these confidences of planetary alliances – pillow talk almost certainly by this time in the narrative – was then instructed to invite him to America for a meeting with other members of the Mercurian fraternity, possibly, although not assuredly, to include the priests who were reputed to be able to visit earth pretty much at will and concomitantly to make a substantial contribution to parish funds. In order to make the financial transaction sound less burdensome, the visit had been described as a 'journey of affiliation'. Ganson took off oversea.

Disillusionment set in not that long after touch-down. Once the money had been handed over, the bed side of things was sharply withdrawn. Within three months Ganson was back in England, his tail between his legs, 'where,' the Master of Peterhouse was heard to remark at High Table, 'it should have stayed in the first place.' Ganson found he'd been given the push. Dismissal had not come about because of any immorality on his part, as might have been expected, in Aldhouse's words, 'for an inappropriate emotional response' to the overtures of a fey American undergraduate but because, in his efforts to drum up sufficient funds to satisfy the Mercurian exchequer, he had sold off some of the college's property as well as his own. 'To put it bluntly, theft,' Aldhouse said. 'That's what got him the sack.' For a while, he had found a job schoolmastering in a castle town favoured by racegoers and day-trippers. Here was housed his college for further education.

Ganson was constantly on the lookout for a second wife, or, more likely, after being let off the hook by the death of his first one, was at liberty to pursue, despite its calamitous outcome, the Casanovian lifestyle that had inspired his liaison with his young American. His had not been true love, as mine had been, for one person and one person alone in the whole wide world for always and always. This is not said boastfully. It had taken years, half the number of years Ganson had been urging me to remarry, to recover from the devastation of Ann's death. For some time after our wives' fatal car crash I had lost touch with my school friend. When I was first admitted to hospital, 'put away,' as my mother-in-law had it, Ganson came to see me and when I reappeared in the world I kept up acquaintance with the man who had been kind enough to have paid me regular visits in the institution I had made my home. Indeed it was he who insisted to my incarcerators that I should be discharged.

Dr du Sautoy had begun my final consultation in his usual style, opening with an inconsequential remark either to break the ice on a relationship never to be labelled as cordial or by this sort of throwaway line to deduce from my reply some indication of improvement – come to that, of deterioration – in my mental condition.

'I think,' Dr du Sautoy said, confiding his mental processes as a way of pushing things along, 'you know a man called Ganson.'

I said I did know Ganson. He paid that no attention.

'A patient was sent to me yesterday, Mr Saunders,' he went on, 'about whom I noticed an unusual feature. He had very dirty wrists. What do you make of that?'

I wondered whether du Sautoy took dirty wrists for a sign of serious illness or of mere absentmindedness and then recalled that Arthur Rimbaud – in a letter I thought and not a piece of poetry – had something to say about dirty wrists. I could not recall whether he referred to the bare skin or to the cuffs of a shirt belonging to someone he was talking about. Possibly to Rimbaud himself, not famous for his over-cleanliness. I mentioned this.

As was his habit, du Sautoy showed no interest whatsoever in what I had said and sat in silence, looking over his glasses in what seemed the contemplation of the good sense or foolishness or even the insanity that had brought me under his care, surrounding the comment I had just made, finally raising his eyes from his desk and repeating his words, 'I think.' Then he went off on a completely different tack.

'I think... we are ready to release you into the community.'

'You make me sound like a nerve gas.'

Du Sautoy puffed a breath of air through tightened lips in acknowledgment that a pleasantry had found favour within a constitution not given to revealing amusement on any level whatsoever. Here was good news both in overcoming his habit of never cracking a smile and for the chance of having another go at life in the outside world. I had come to view du Sautoy with suspicion. At least, I disliked the glasses he wore, a sign perhaps of returning health in that a concept of any kind, even one of rather negative substance, had begun to stir in the murky indifference of a mind in shock. Doctors' glasses as a general rule take on a sophistication rarely seen in other circles, not always worn across the eyes but propped on the forehead or on the tip of the nose, dangled from a cord, the lenses extra large or small, the framing more austere. My feeling in those days was that if they were good at their job doctors shouldn't need glasses at all. Of course it might be that their lenses had been ground in laboratories unavailable to the general public which enabled them to detect the nature of a patient's illness as the glasses – when correctly aligned – bored into him from across their desks. It was possible these bespoke lenses could discern the colour of the patient's etheric double, according to a distant cousin of mine an adjunct of the physical body common to us all, although invisible except to initiates, the miscolouring of which could lead to physical – and mental – disorders.

Du Sautoy enquired whether Ganson would be able to keep an eye on me in the early days of freedom when I would still be finding my feet. He kindly took the job on.

On our river walk that morning, Ganson took the opportunity to remark, as he had often remarked before, that I should think of re-marrying, of removing my son from his grandparents and bringing him up myself. In my turn, I repeated, as I had often repeated before, my immunity to human affection passively as well as actively, this time using in illustration a poem I had come across somewhere:

> Now heaven be thanked, I am out of love again!
> I have been long a slave, and now am free;
> I have been tortured, and am eased of pain;
> I have been blind, and now my eyes can see;
> I have been lost, and now the way lies plain;
> I have been caged, and now I hold the key;
> I have been mad, and now at last am sane;
> I am wholly I, that was but a half of me.
> So, a free man, my dull proud path I plod,
> Who, tortured, blind, mad, caged, was once a God.

Ganson was impressed. 'That's not bad. Who wrote it?'

I told him. 'I've never heard of the woman. Still, I wonder if that's not all to the good.' He linked an arm in mine and, deep in thought, walked us through paludinal grasses to the bank of the river. Water lapped against slimy stones to which small inedible molluscs had attached themselves. Ganson dislodged one with the toe of his shoe. It sank, making a sucking noise. 'Sunk without trace,' Ganson said. 'Sunk without trace.' He was not talking about the displaced mussel which sent up a final bubble of despair from the river bed. 'You've given me an idea. Something that will give the Academy a shot in the arm.'

I saw at once I had made a terrible mistake. I had unwittingly initi-ated, and unless I could very quickly dissuade Ganson from further contemplation of the matter, would have to take sole responsibility for an innovation in Academy affairs Ganson always referred to by this particular phrase. Ganson's 'shots in the arm' nearly always resulted in inconvenience to members of staff, to students as well even if, as had sometimes to be conceded, they resulted in a benefit to one side or another, to both on occasion.

These innovations were not necessarily improvements in academic achievements. For instance, there had been a plan to award the Academy a coat of arms, the application brusquely turned down by the College of Heralds. Ganson had had to make do with commissioning a striped necktie for the men, a scarf for the women, in contrasting colours, which, although not compulsory, students were encouraged to wear when attending classes. Another 'shot' was under consideration, a plan to get rid of the ballet school next door and establish within its area a buffet room for the staff. Following university parlance, Ganson proposed the space would be known either as the Refectory – he accented the first syllable when he used the word – or the Buttery. No progress had been made with this scheme, either because the Principal of the attached school had dug in her heels or more probably because the relevant documents had been shredded by Colin Bailey who, foreseeing the extra work involved, had blocked its implementation. 'A shot,' he had summed it up, 'more in the foot than in the arm.'

'Sunk Without Trace,' Project SWOT, as Ganson had named it, was about to be put into service, explaining today's symposium to which science and humanities teachers in our small college, too small to boast a common room and without its proposed refectory necessitating our recourse to a public house, had been summoned to report on which worthy and wrongly forgotten figure in his or her particular discipline was considered worthy of bringing to their students' attention. The plan, our Dean had told us, at the same time as he shamingly credited me with having given him the inspiration, was to arouse interest outside a curriculum perceived as having been on the narrow side up to now and needing in his words, a shot in the arm. Peter Cazalet imitated him well. 'We must encourage our young men and women to wander unaccompanied down bosky pathways of learning as well as marching them along its well-trodden highroads.' Today we were to hear who had chosen who.

Members of staff drifted in, Stephen and Sheila Aldhouse (Art, Media Studies), Peter Cazalet (Spanish), *Maître de conférences* Mariette Caplain-Dol (mathematics), others beside. Bailey greeted each in turn, deploying the conviviality he always put on show in public houses, a virtue unconnected absolutely to alcoholic intake. People's deportment in pubs, however much or little they have had to drink, is not to be construed as reflective of their true social values, good or bad, but, by an infusion of the reputation with which the premises are still to this day associated, an environment of a certain unrespectability – and the enjoinment, 'let's go to the pub,' being suggestive of an excursion into dangerous territory – one finds that pubs are conducive to a more pronounced letting-down of the hair or the moroseness of the solitary drinker than are put on show in other surroundings.

So far as Bailey was concerned, this large-scale bonhomie contrasted violently with the front displayed in his office where he revealed himself as a much less welcoming, not far off hostile, guardian of a space he preferred to maintain unencumbered by visitors. Hands scrabbled for official papers that had been sided on his desk to make way for a computer screen on which horses silently thundered across turf or hurled themselves over fences. This was quickly switched off. A second, not dissimilar, apparatus that displayed complicated charts of runners, riders, owners, betting odds, distances, handicaps, jockeys' colours, sourced from a subscription website most likely financed by Academy funds, was also disconnected. 'I find myself a trifle overstretched today,' Bailey would remark. 'May we by chance reschedule?'

'Ah, the Aldhice, Stephen, Sheila: Peter: *Madame la Docteur.*'

'*Le*, Stairs. *Toujours le.*'

'Oh, jolly good. Welcome to the conflab.'

Somebody offered to buy drinks. Bailey at once put paid to the idea, scooping up our own empty tankards and hurrying them back to the bar counter.

'I think it wiser to be revealed seated at a bare table. The Dean will then be obliged to do the honours.' Bailey gave another of his twitches. Here was an example of our bursar's methodology of juggling expenses: when applied to Academy affairs earning Ganson's commendation for a careful disposal of available funds.

We sat for about five minutes. Then Ganson hurried in. He wore, as always, a tweed jacket and a pair of brown corduroy trousers, either garment a maintainable vector of the aroma of green peppers for ever perpending in his vicinity. He dressed, Aldhouse remarked, 'like an underpaid classics master at a minor prep school under threat of dismissal for rogering the matron.'

'Apologies for lateness. Pressures, pressures.'

As Bailey had foretold, he asked Fred to take orders for drinks all round, limiting himself to a glass of sparkling water in obedience to a regime he was disposed to boast about. 'I never drink in the daytime' he would say, 'but when the shadows lengthen, and the evening comes, and the busy world is hushed, and the fever of life is over, and our work is done, I am not averse to getting rat-arsed.'

These protestations that he did not drink alcohol until nightfall were not to be taken seriously, although 'rat-arsed' as a description of the form of the inebriation with which, at whatever time of day or night, he was now and then overcome, was taking things too far. He could certainly prove obstreperous, usually about some modern institutions, the mobile telephone, for example, or a lapse in grammar he found irritating: a word in his ear usually enough to quieten him down.

'Where's Scottie?'

Ganson referred to a relative newcomer in our ranks, Scott McLeod, R. S. (Religious Studies), the man Ganson was anxious should not get to hear of his spiritualistic experiments as a schoolboy. I got on well with McLeod. Tall, thin, neat brown beard, prematurely bald, holding himself well up to his full height, he resembled a royal personage in late Victorian, perhaps Edwardian, days, because of some scandal or an early, conjecturally syphilitic, death passed over in history books of the period. He was keen on sports, of what nature it mattered not at all so long as it produced some violent exercise. He played cricket in the summer and was a useful opening batsman but the game was not strenuous enough for him and when he was put out to pasture on the boundary or ran quick singles he dreamed of the winter days to come when he could hack a football, brandish a hockey stick or throw himself about in a game of rugby. If there were no team game for him to compete in, he'd go swimming or mountaineering or riding or fly off to the ski-slopes. Each one of these activities had on occasion resulted in accidents, a blow on the arm from a cricket ball, an awkward tackle in a touch-down, a tumble in the Alps, mishaps sometimes serious enough to lay him off duty.

Ganson's question needed careful answering. Scottie McLeod was in gaol. A few weeks ago out riding with the local hunt he had slashed a saboteur across the face with his riding crop. The magistrate had issued what she called 'a sharp corrective' of a month in prison, a sentence that, with remission, was hardly long enough, as Cazalet had remarked, to sew a mailbag. He was in fact due out tomorrow. Luckily the incident had occurred at half-term so, until now, he had not been missed.

Ganson answered his own question: 'Done himself another mischief, I suppose. Never mind. We can get along without him.'

I wondered which belief McLeod would choose that had 'sunk without trace' and considered worth investigating in the series of lectures Ganson had planned across the academic spectrum. Mithraism came to mind, Ophiolatreia, Theosophy. The last was a creed devotedly followed by a niece of my mother-in-law's who was always keen to convert others to a faith that seemed outworn enough for academic study in McLeod's tutorials. I'd ask him when he was at liberty whether he thought it worthy of consideration.

'Ladies, gentlemen, let us commence.' Ganson tugged at a ginger beard, another possible source of the vegetal miasma with which he was surrounded.

'Dean, would you mind if I kicked off?' Aldhouse asked. 'I'm a bit short of time.'

'Time, Stephen, what is time?' Ganson asked. 'I don't have time to smoke a gasper, I don't have time for a bite of lunch, I don't have time to do cuckies. Go on, then. And don't tell me you've plumped for that Brunery johnny you make such a song and dance about.'

'No, Dean. I admit to having a soft spot for Brunery and the anti-clerical school of art. However, I've chosen an Englishman, Stanhope Forbes. The name probably means nothing to you.'

Ganson was ruffled by Aldhouse's suggestion of a gap in his knowledge of the history of English painting and its exponents with which, as he waved his hand, he indicated he was widely familiar.

'The Newlyn school. *Plein air*, that sort of thing. I think I may claim a nodding acquaintance with the Newlyn school.' Ganson rattled off a few names: 'Thomas Gotch, Henry Scott Tuke, Chevalier Tayler.'

'Full marks,' Aldhouse said.

That didn't go down well either. 'You're not talking to a schoolboy, Stephen. You'd better cut along then since you're in such a hurry.' He turned to Mme Caplain-Dol on whom it was thought he had a crush. 'Mariette, my dear, you next. Have you selected your figure from the world of mathematics past?'

'*Mais oui*. I shall be lecturing on the Cambridge professor, Walter

William Rouse Ball, eighteen-fifty to nineteen-twenty-five. You have probably never heard of him but that is the point of the seminar, *n'est ce pas.*

'Wasn't he the chap who solved Kirkman's problem of the fifteen schoolgirls?' Cazalet asked.

'No, Peter, Kirkman himself solved that.'

'Speaking personally,' Bailey said, 'I do not see myself as having much of a problem with fifteen schoolgirls.' He gave another of his twitches.

Mme Caplain-Dol ignored this. 'You are right though in thinking Kirkman was of the same era. All Ball did was to include the problem in his well-known *Mathematical Recreations and Essays*, eighteen ninety-two, a book that has never since been out of print. He made no significant contribution to the science of mathematics unlike Kirkman, Thomas Penyngton Kirkman, eighteen hundred and six to eighteen ninety-five, but he made a laudable effort, at the end a thwarted one, to publish a variorum edition of Newton's *Principia*, sixteen eighty-seven. If he had managed it, it would have been a worthy landmark to a career he dedicated instead to the welfare of his students. He was a wonderful friend to Trinity, where he spent most of his life. He built the undergraduates a cricket pavilion. *Hélas, dans ces jours, c'est un pissoir.* And a billiard-room, which is not. And instituted a junior common-room. There is a funny story about that. One of the students asked another what he thought of the scheme and by whom it had been initiated. His informant said, "I believe the idea is all Ball's." '

'Oh, very droll,' Bailey said, 'Keep it in for the second house.'

I asked what Kirkman's problem had been. Mariette began a rundown.

'Fifteen girls at boarding school take their daily walk three abreast. How can it be arranged so that each girl walks in the same row with every other...oh, *un moment.*' She got up and went over to a thickset man who had just come into the pub. It was Drake, the person who ate breakfast in the café above which I lived. We had spoken occasionally when he always presented himself as an infinitely lugubrious figure deeply discontented with his job of chauffeur – other tasks may have been allotted – to a person of extreme wealth or so it looked from the prestigious car in which this man drove his master on mainly local expeditions. We had often acknowledged each other, once or twice passed a few words, interrupted usually by Drake's having to leave for duties in no possible way offering job satisfaction. 'No peace for the wicked,' he would say as he got up and plodded mournfully on his way. Recently he had been sitting hunched over a book, always the same one, following the letters with a forefinger, occasionally muttering to himself, when finished marking his place with a silk bookmark as he rose to take his place once more in the ranks of the labouring classes. His text, printed upon India paper and enclosed in a limp black binding, proposed it to be the Bible or the Koran, some other text of dense religious constitution. On the morning I'm going to describe, he looked up when I came in and beckoned me over.

'Do you happen to speak German, squire?'

'A bit.'

'Do you know what *Schenke* means? It doesn't give it in my dictionary.'

Oddly enough, the word was one with which, at school, I had dazzled my German master when translating some passage or other from an author I'd forgotten.

'Bright of you, Saunders. How do you come to know that?'

It would not have been politic to mention that it was an exhortation from the spirit world that I should work harder at my German studies as the goad that had fixed in me this particular shard of knowledge. I shrugged my shoulders.

'Natural genius, sir.'

Drake smiled at my story. I suggested that 'café' might do. 'Maybe "inn". It depends on the context.'

Drake handed me the book, open at the title-page spread. On the left a frontispiece reproduced a leaf of what looked like Arabian manuscript. On the right in an elaborate black letter font Drake's source was spelled out. It was the *West-östlicher Divan* of Johann von Goethe.

The poetry is not Goethe's best. Dr Muller, the Academy's German professor to whom I had rarely spoken, may have recommended it to his class as an example of the influence of an eastern poetry collection, the Divan of the title, on the intellect of Germany's greatest poet, a co-alition that, in modern terms, social as much as literary, could be used to point up the benefit of an harmonious co-existence between disparate nations. A poet, Edward Dowden, had made a fist of translating Goethe's version into rhymed English. For *Schenke* he had had Tavern:

> Yes, in the tavern I too have been seated.
> For me, as for the rest, the wine was meted.

21

Now I saw the context, it was clear that *Schenke* ought to be translated as 'divan', meaning in this instance a wine-shop or a smoking establishment. The word would be more amusingly transcribed as *diwan*, imparting the implicit loucheness associated with sanctuaries offering recreations other than wine and tobacco and, at the same time, playing on Goethe's use of it in his title where it meant simply a poetic anthology. I put this to Drake as the best that could be managed. He thanked me and shut the book with a snap as if dismissing for the day any further intellectual cudgeling. On this particular morning, he had not been called to arms as early as usual and we went briefly over each other's life history. Both of us turned out to be descended from circus families. A far distant ancestor of mine had been a tightrope walker. Drake's grandfather had been billed as The Man Who Can Lift a Horse. 'He could do no such thing,' the grandson reported. 'Well, he could but not with his bare hands. He used a sort of hoist thing with ropes and pulleys and the smallest fucking horse you ever saw, more like a dog really, a Shetland pony, I suppose or a Dartmoor one.'

Mariette returned to her seat.

'Is that your latest conquest, Mariette,' Bailey asked.

Mme Caplain-Dol rounded on him indignantly, plucking Mrs Aldhouse's spoon from the saucer of her coffee cup and rapping Bailey over the knuckles: '*Merde*, Stairs, a pupil only and not my department either. *En tous cas, je m'ennuie avec les queues britanniques.*' She turned to me. 'Going back to Rouse Ball, you'd have been a fan of his. He was a keen amateur, *qu'est ce qu'on dit en anglais, escamoteur?* Conjuror, *c'est ça.* He started a magical society for Cambridge men, the Pentacle Club.'

'It's my son who's the conjuror, not I.'

Mrs Aldhouse evinced interest in George's hobby.

'Do you think your son might like to come and do a magic show at my daughter's birthday party?'

'I'm afraid he doesn't live with me.'

The Dean looked up from his water glass. 'Well, he ought to, as I've told him a million times before.'

The inquisition continued. I was the last to be questioned.

'Leonard, that woman's poem you quoted? Is she to be your chosen Sunk without Tracer?'

'No. I thought for a long time about possible candidates: Tessimond, Frankau, Noyes, Humbert Wolfe, J. K. Stephen.'

'Never heard of any of them.'

'Isn't that rather the point? The forgotten middlebrow poets shunned by the academics, out of print at the booksellers? Anyway at last I decided. I've chosen Adam Lindsay Gordon.'

'The horse-riding jackaroo. Mid nineteenth-century. Suicided if I remember rightly.'

'He wasn't Australian. His parents made him emigrate. He briefly joined the police; left the force and became a horse breaker; then his mother, who had never liked him, kicked the bucket and he came into a bit of money. He stood for parliament for a while, got bored with that, lost his money, rode in races to try and make ends meet, had expectations of a Scottish inheritance. Those hopes were stymied by lawyers of the Bleak House variety, resulting in depression and then he killed himself, as you say, Dean. Sadly enough, on the day a book of his poems came out. He was the first person to write bush ballads. He was thought of highly enough for there to be a bust of him in Poets' Corner. I've always had a soft spot for Gordon, even at his worst and he is often that. His "How We Beat the Favourite" was the first poem I ever read: for pleasure, that is. I used to bicycle around the countryside reciting it out loud.'

'I remember that bike of yours,' Ganson went on. 'Flashy, lot of gears. We were all green with envy. Can you give us a short poetic sample?'

'This is from *How We Beat*.'

> She passed like an arrow Kildare and Cock Sparrow,
> And Mantrap and Mermaid refused the stone wall;
> And Giles on The Grayling came down at the paling,
> And I was left sailing in front of them all.

'Doggerel,' Ganson said. 'Sub Banjo Paterson. Your seminars will bring disgrace upon the Academy.'

'As a racing man,' Bailey said, 'I can see the jingle has merit.'

Ganson had snatched away my copy of Gordon's poems and was leafing through it: 'Godfrey Daniel Simpson, listen to this:

> Weird pictures arise, quaint devices,
> Rude emblems, baked funeral meats,

Didn't someone say that before?

> Strong incense, rare wines, and rich spices,
> The ashes, the shrouds, and the sheets;
> Does our thraldom fall short of completeness
> For the magic of a charnel-house charm,
> And the flavour of a poisonous sweetness,
> And the odour of a poisonous balm?

This is awful stuff.'

'What about this from the same poem?':

> Man's works are graven, cunning, and skilful
> On earth, where his tabernacles are;
> But the sea is wanton, the sea is wilful,
> And who shall mend her and who shall mar?
> Shall we carve success or record disaster
> On the bosom of her heaving alabaster?
> Will her purple pulse beat fainter or faster
> For fallen sparrow or fallen star?

Ganson was unimpressed. 'Something has gone sadly awry with the versification. "Heaving alabaster", forsooth. I didn't expect you to sink quite so low.'

He was about to hand the book back when his eyes fell on an inscription on the flyleaf: ' "To a young pal from an old 'un, T. Scott." Was he your schoolmaster?'

'Godfather.'

'Clergyman too, I wouldn't wonder, judging by the lines he's written underneath your name:

> God who created me nimble and light of limb
> In three elements free, to run, to ride, to swim;
> Now when the sense is dim,
> but now from the heart of joy,
> I would remember Him;
> take the thanks of a boy.

That's not Gordon? No, not nearly bad enough. Well, you've made your bed and you must lie on it. I can't say I approve from the little I've read today.' Ganson began to sing to the tune of *Frère Jacques*:

Shakespeare, Milton,
Shakespeare,Milton,
Shelley as well,
Shelley as well.
Adam Lindsay Gordon,
Adam Lindsay Gordon,
Ethel M. Dell.

I suppose it would appear invidious for you to teach my own small contribution to the literary world?'

Ganson had published two collections of verses. *Balls to Mr Bangelstein* and *Feeble My Lays* appeared more or less simultaneously although under different, provincial, imprints. They had been reviewed together by *The Times Literary Supplement*, categorising them as of the smoking-room school of verse and (more kindly) nominating Ganson as a 'Calverley for our times.'

'Invidious and also irrelevant. You have not sunk without trace.'

'Kind of you to say so. Well, I must be off if we're all finished.' Ganson slapped his thigh, setting off his personal aroma of simmering ratatouille. 'Are you going back to the office, Stairs?'

Bailey looked up, surprised at being addressed. 'Er, no, Dean, I shall remain here a little longer if I may, have a quick rub-down with the *Sporting Times* and partake of one of Frederick's Garden of Eden pies.' He indicated the news-sheet open across the table. Some runners had been marked with a red pencil.

Ganson tolerated Bailey's betting perhaps because his acquaintance with the turf was reputed to swell the institute's coffers or at least to balance the books despite depletions needed to instigate these chancy accumulations. Of course there was no absolute guarantee that Bailey would not gamble away every penny piece in the Academy's bank account. Ganson must have given some thought to that and considered the risk worth taking.

Certainly, up to now, no such catastrophe had occurred. That was not to say money was never tight. Occasions arose when bills were outstanding: salaries put on hold: textbooks and computer software returned to the suppliers for re-order at a later date. To give him his due, Bailey readily admitted these exigencies. Any defalcation attributable to the bursar's office was laid fairly and squarely on the table with a disclosure, unblushingly advanced, that we were faced with 'a minor hiccough.'

As we went out, Ganson turned to me: 'Did Mariette say *queues britanniques?*

'Yes.'

'Not *coeurs?*'

'I don't think so.'

'Neither do I. Um.'

Ganson pulled ruminatively at his beard. He may have been giving thought to the Doctor's qualifying as a candidate for his affections despite her satiety of British suitors or, again, whether she had already taken her turn, counting him among those responsible for current exhaustion of desire. It was never absolutely unrewarding to conjecture that any woman at all passing across Ganson's vision had been romantically eyed up: some of them approached: wooed: added to his list of conquests. What was more certain was that the affairs, if affairs they became, were short-lived. Within a few weeks, Ganson, his egg head shining, his beard fierier than usual, would announce, usually in the pub, that the liaison was at an end. The search for amiable companionship was back on. In the most recent case, that of the Academy's dancing-mistress, Madam Tumbleova to give her Ganson's nickname, the relationship had been of a stormy constitution, one to bear comparison with that of Fred the publican and his wife.

The *contretemps* was kept alive to this day. As mentioned, Ganson had named his institution AHEAD. A flag with these letters painted across the pages of an open book fluttered over the main entrance. The first three letters stood for Academy of Higher Education. The last two, although they gave the impression to outsiders of the Academy's thrustful approach to learning, in fact represented the words 'And Dance.' Attached to our premises was a dancing school. It was under the supervision of one of Ganson's women friends, called I think Carol Smith but because he now held her in poor estate renamed Tumbleova to specify at one and the same time the Russian nation's love of ballet and the directress's inability at interpreting that particular art form on any acceptable level.

This hostility had been assumed by Ganson after her refusal to be ousted from her premises by her admirer, a tenacity made keener most likely when she came to understand that the only reason for Ganson's ever having paid her court in the first place was because he wanted to commandeer her section of the building for his own purposes. Ganson found it particularly galling that through a wall of the room he had made his private office could be heard the music of a piano, Tumbleova's shouted instructions, and the thump of young, dancing, feet.

'Can I give you a lift?'

'No, it's only round the corner.'

'Nonsense, it's at least a quarter of an hour's walk. Hop in.'

'Aren't I taking you out of your way?'

Ganson didn't answer that question. Over the years, after we'd had dinner, come out of a cinema, been to the pub, he had always been anxious to set me on my road by calling a taxi or putting me on a bus. Once I had taken this for solicitousness, a worry on his part that I had drunk too much, overeaten, was still dazed from the film we'd watched, afflicted with some incapacity or other sufficient to upset my sense of direction and keep me wandering the streets for hours on end, but over the years I had come to the conclusion he was anxious only to ensure I was out of his sight before he set off on a secret pursuit of his own which, if he offered even a hint of the direction he was heading, might give away an assignation almost certainly involving a woman. It could be that, when he'd dropped me off, he was going to beat a retreat back to the Jolly Herring and patch things up with our doctor of mathematics.

As he started up his engine, he asked one more question: 'Why does Stairs call them 'Garden of Eden Pies?'

'Because when you've 'ad 'em you 'eave.'

CHAPTER II

'Don't think I'm earwigging or anything, but I couldn't help but hear what you were saying.'

The woman at the writing-desk pivoted on a swivel chair to speak to my mother and myself having tea behind her. Being then of an imaginative age, I gave thought to this colourful person's performing a few more revolutions, spinning ever faster and then, as she peeled herself from her perch, launching into a high-kicking dance routine, revealing lacy underwear. A comprehensive brightness of turn-out, a summer frock printed with poppies riotously in bloom, red high heels, livid lipstick, a hat of more adventurous proportions than the one worn by my mother who had received – and obeyed – my instructions on the necessity, if she wore a hat at all, of choosing one of the very simplest design, proposed to me the possibility of some stage business to be rehearsed on the hotel carpet.

It was school speech day, 1990. I was thirteen. Formalities were over, to mutual relief. My mother had flown over from Germany where my father was stationed to take me out for the tea which had been laid in front of us.

'I wish we could get over more. Daddy misses you terribly. You have made friends, haven't you? Promise me you're not lonely.'

It was at that moment that, with a sheet of flame from the poppies on her dress, the woman had whirled round to address us.

'I hope I'm not pushin' in. My husband the Major and I are resident in this hotel you know, now that he has retired from his senior bursary positions. If your son feels lonely, we would be only too pleased to invite him over here for his lunch one Sunday if he would care to come at all.'

She came over and shook our hands. Nails were polished to match the shoes. Bangles jangled on a plump wrist.

'Emily Saunders. How very very kind of you. Darling, isn't that kind of Mrs – er?'

'Scott. April Scott.' Mrs Scott gripped her knees in her hands and bent beaming down on me. 'Oh, what a nice boy you look. I could just about eat you up.'

My mother felt called upon to adjust Mrs Scott's estimate: 'Not as nice as he could be sometimes, I'm afraid.'

Mrs Scott acknowledged the likelihood of a qualification. 'Boys will be boys,' she said. She patted my hand. A drink was offered by one of the women to the other. Play was made of its being 'a tiny bit early,' establishing a liaison flourishing over the sherry schooners. I took a pull of Cydrax and considered the situation.

Sunday invitations had their ups and downs. It had to be said that the hotel food was pretty good, its weekend lunches rather a speciality. My mother said they had a way with gravy. Against that, as the guest of two grown-up strangers, it would entail putting on one's best suit, a clean shirt, the school tie, sensible shoes, and being on one's best behaviour. More worrying still was that a Sunday lunch invitation would interrupt routine. Sunday afternoons were given up to raising the dead.

There were four of us: myself, Ganson, Amos, Atkinson. Meetings were held in a small room known as the Boot-Hole, the exclusive province of the boilerman, Brill, first name never disclosed, who did not work at weekends. Brill was a being of infinite pessimism. When we passed Brill as he mopped the passages with a bucket of water he had infused with a powerful disinfectant as a preventative against the germs he believed all boys unexceptionally carried and with which he could by laid low unless stringent hygienic precautions were imposed our custom was to give him the time of day. 'Morning, Brill.' 'Morning, sir,' Brill would reply. 'Nice day,' we would say. After this brief engagement, Brill took the opportunity of putting his monumental gloominess on show. 'Won't last.' That was his invariable reply. Atkinson had added the words of this exchange to those of a folk-song taught to the youngest boys at the school, *A Keeper Would A' hunting Go*. The chorus goes:

'Jackie boy.'
'Master?
'Sing ye well?'
'Very well.'
Hey down, Ho down,
Derry-derry-down
Among the leaves so green-o.

Akky's version ran:

'Morning, Brill.'
'Morning, sir.'

'Nice day.'
'Won't last.'
Hey down, ho down,
Derry-derry down
Among the leaves so green-o.

I mention this only because the theme of animal pursuit in the antiquated song we had sung as new boys to the notes hammered out on a piano by the mistress in charge of the bottom form had pierced the heart of the then seven-year-old Andrew Amos, the self-appointed leader of our psychical research group, as keenly as the arrows of the song had pierced the flesh of the hunted deer within the gamekeeper's arboreal preserve. Amos had been so violently repelled by the bloodthirsty pursuit of the 'merry little doe among the leaves so green-o' that he had forsworn for six years now the eating of animal flesh.

For our parleys with the deceased, we relied to begin with on the movement of a card table once used for mahjong, now requisitioned for our own purposes. We sat in a circle, fingers touching as they rested on the baize surface. If the table tilted to the left it signified that the spirits of the departed had given us a positive answer to our question, the right advancing a negative. Enquiries related for the most part to school life. Would the school win the match on Saturday? Were we correct in thinking we would be examined on the French Revolution with especial reference to Talleyrand? Was our maths master to all intents and purposes clinically insane?

Because I was interested in conjuring I had read somewhere that table-turning seems to work because the participants are hoping either for a yes or a no to a particular concern and therefore are subconsciously exerting pressure, left or right, to extract the expected reply. I put this to the group. It was agreed a new system must be found. We discovered in Brill's lair an abandoned wooden knife-sharpener which we set on its side. The handle was then spun around, coming to rest on the letters of the alphabet we had pasted around the perimeter of the machine's wooden casing. At first, before we oiled the interior mechanism, the handle was inclined to stop twice in succession at the letter L, often at the beginning of a word. This prompted Ganson, already, some thirty years before this story begins, presenting himself as a bit of a wag, to suggest that it must be a person of Welsh origin who was 'coming through.'

Then we progressed to the Ring and the Disc. A gold wedding ring belonging to Amos's grandmother which he explained had fallen from a finger emaciated by age and presented to him in advance of her impending decease was suspended on a piece of cotton over a circle of letters from a Scrabble bag. This system increased the speed of messaging from the beyond, at the same time adding to its complexity.

Amos, to whom we deferred on most occult matters, pointed out that each of our divergent sun signs was equatable with one of the four elements. 'Ganson is fiery, Saunders is earthy, Atkinson is watery, I am airy. We are therefore equipped to deal with any elemental beings who may introduce themselves, the elves, the gnomes, the sylphs, and the undines.' A suggestion of mine that we might begin with the undines, said to possess feminine allure, a quality to which we were becoming alerted, was seconded by Ganson who asked: 'What do they wear undine-neath?'

Flippancy of this kind, indulged every so often in periods, often lengthy ones, of non-communication from beyond the veil, was frowned on by Amos whose asceticism, reflected in his vegetarian regime, bore some relation to the prophet's whose name he bore in a mutually stern disapproval of luxurious living of all kinds, of those 'that lie upon beds of ivory, and stretch themselves upon their couches... that drink wine in bowls.'

One Sunday our communicant offered a clue to his identity. The ring spelt out the letters 'r. s. puden.' I suggested Rice Pudding, immediately dismissed by Amos as an impropriety of the grossest nature. Mr Pudding gave out that he would soon disclose his real name. True to his word, at our next séance, Atkinson said he heard a strange voice in his head. He sounded strange himself, speaking in deeper tones than usual – he was the only one of us whose voice had broken – and added a rider to the effect that our visitor was in future to be known as Gregory, Gregory Rice Pudding. He assumed a foreign accent when he said this. Amos produced the answer to this enigma: 'Our communicant is Grigori Yefimovich Rasputin.' The wild-eyed monk of Tsarist Russia had got in touch. This had to be accounted as something of a *succès d'estime*, at least in spiritualist circles, usually having to rely on an inglorious range of advisers, more often than not of Chinese or Red Indian origin. On a practical level, on the other hand, the advice Rasputin had to offer, although never as cataclysmic as it had been in the case of the Romanovs, left a good deal to be desired. A method recommended for dodging physical training classes was found to be deeply flawed, a suggestion that Atkinson should play wing three-quarter in a rugby match rather than in the scrum turned out disastrously for the house fifteen. His prediction that if I paid more attention to my German studies I'd be 'donated a gift' had yet to be fulfilled.

One Sunday, the Scrabble letters spelled out a message from Rasputin to the effect that our communication system was out of date. 'No more ring plus disc,' the *staretz* commanded, 'Blanken minds and I will speak through thee' (or 'them,' the message was unclear and it seemed not worth while to ask for a repeat) 'each in turn.' The abandonment of selfhood in order to allow to enter consciousness the personality of Gregory, as Rasputin had said he preferred to be called, resulted, for my part and I suspect the others', in saying the first thing that came into our heads. Accusations of trickery began to be levelled one against the other, accusations which I was later to learn had plagued the spiritualist movement almost from the day of its inception.

Now that it was no longer necessary to read the Scrabble letters or to take notes on their formation into words, it was thought we might benefit by holding our meetings in the dark. Looked at from Rasputin's viewpoint, a darkened room reflected to some extent the blankness of mind necessary for the reception of his messages. This worked well to a certain extent but, mirroring the gloom in which we sat, Gregory's utterances grew ever more obscure. Whether or not he recognized our different makeups, that each of us represented one of the four elements as Amos had observed at one of our earliest conclaves, earth, air, fire, and water, so that, for instance, when an answer arrived through Atkinson it advised violent action, as opposed to Amos's cloaking what might have been practical guidance in an air of mystery, remained unknown. When my turn came around, I was nervous that I'd be unable to hear anything at all and, if that were the case, be obliged to invent a plausible item of news. It soon became clear that Rasputin's wish to use the group as vehicles for his messages was sowing discontent. Everyone owned up that he occasionally cheated. Even so, some of Rasputin's advice, if it were Rasputin's and not our own, had borne fruit. For instance I had gone to the top of my German class, an achievement the master percipiently remarked could be attributed only to supernatural intercession. Nevertheless, a sweeping change was required.

'We are all corrupt,' Amos announced. 'We must find a virgin seer, a neutral vehicle, preferably junior to ourselves and able to be bossed about, for Gregory to use as his own.'

Amos, who had been reading *The Moonstone*, went on to refer to the episode of the Indian fakirs and a small boy who had ink poured into the palm of his hand, enabling him to gaze into the future. Atkinson remarked that we were all small boys.

'Yes,' Amos said, 'but we're not Indian. And we're not that small.'

I pointed out that there was no Indian boy at the school.

'There's Jayawickrama.'

'He's Sri Lankan.'

'He's Eastern though; and the Eastern races are renowned for their physical aptitudes.'

Rasputin approved the use of Jayawickrama to act as his go-between and confirmed that the method mentioned in *The Moonstone* might be adopted. 'You see many things in nick,' he radioed. 'Nick' had been interpreted as 'ink.'

I had to excuse myself from attendance at the séance where Jayawickrama was to make his debut because of the promised invitation to lunch from Major and Mrs Scott. They were sitting in armchairs reading the Sunday papers. Mrs Scott was no less gaudily got up than when I had first seen her. The Major wore a tweed jacket, cavalry twill trousers, a woollen tie. His shaggy grey moustache seemed not to fit an otherwise closely barbered face, almost to be a stage accoutrement purchased from a shop such as the one where I bought my conjuring tricks until, as the day progressed, I came to see it had been grown to disguise, or rather to fail to disguise, a pair of prominent front teeth. Mrs Scott introduced us.

'Splendid that you could come along,' the Major said. 'As you observe, Mrs Scott's partaking of a glass of sherry before we repair to the dining-room for what I hope will turn out a decent spread. They usually do one well of a Sunday. I myself never take strong waters and neither I'm sure do you. Ha. We'll both have a glass of squash at the table. Come along, April, we're going in now. Bring your drink with you. Don't spill it, my dear. You sit here, Leonard, where you can survey the room and tell us if there's anyone you like better than yourself. Now, let's see what's running in the Grub Stakes.' He opened a menu and rubbed his hands vigorously together as if washing them at a basin.

The Scotts gave full attention to the food put in front of them, absolving me from replying to the sort of questions I thought they might have been disposed to ask on school life in all its aspects. We ate our way through mushroom soup, roast lamb, peas, cauliflower, potatoes, the joint carved at the table.

'Remember, Leonard, always tip the carver,' the Major said in a rare moment of speech. He helped himself to mint sauce. 'Eat hearty.'

Apple pie followed the meat. I asked if I were allowed not to have custard. I'd always disliked custard. This worried my mother who believed, justifiably, that it would prove a staple of boarding-school diet. 'Try to like custard' was one of three admonitions she had offered when, five years ago, she'd said goodbye at the school gates: 'Call the masters Sir, try to like custard, and never play the cut shot to an off-break bowler.'

'Not like custard, Lennie?' Mrs Scott said. 'Aren't you funny.'

'If he doesn't want custard, he needn't have it,' the Major said, beaming across at me and revealing his rabbit teeth. 'It's his day and he must do exactly what he wants.' The hands were washed again as the pie was set before him.

After lunch, Mrs Scott suggested we should have a 'little outing.' The Major agreed. A place of interest was decided upon. The Major brought the car round; and what a car it was. Its beauty astonished me. Three or four years ago I had taken an interest in old cars and in one of my books now discarded to make room for conjuring manuals, a hobby itself superseded by that of the occult, there had been a picture of this exact model. Major Scott seemed delighted that I was able to identify the machine, to give it its name, *La déesse*, and to point out that General de Gaulle had always ridden in a Citroën of similar design which, because of its superior suspension, I added, had saved him from assassination.

'Correct on all points,' the Major said, with a display of the teeth. 'Ten out of ten. Now, we two will scramble into the back. Mrs Scott can do the driving. And I shouldn't wonder,' he said as we settled down, 'but if one day when you're a bit older and we can find a place where we're not overlooked, you shouldn't have a turn behind the wheel.'

Here was excitement on a grand scale: to be allowed within the next few years to drive any make of car, let alone this white futuristic monster, was a completely unexpected outcome of this formal luncheon.

I turned over in my mind how this car could be best exploited until the time came when I could take my place in the driver's seat: that is to say, if the Scotts issued another Sunday invitation, how to persuade them to collect me from school rather than my getting the bus to their hotel. My friends would be alerted to this rendezvous by the sound of the car's distinctly Gallic klaxon that would blast out across the playground like the massed rams-horns of the biblical priests of old, shaking the school's foundations and crowding the boys to the windows from where I would be seen, hands in the pockets of my best shorts, sensible shoes brightly polished, casually strolling towards the great limousine whose beating engine they could hear through the glass they had steamed over with their admiring breath.

A boy, Amos, for choice, recognizing at last that my qualities were equal if not superior to his own, would subserviently use the sleeve of his blazer to clear the misted windowpanes for me to be the better observed as I awaited the opening of the front passenger door either by Mrs Scott or, because one could not be at all certain that she would pass muster if arrayed in one of her flowery dresses or, heaven forbid, be wearing a hat, preferably by the Major himself. Then I would swing myself inside, pull the door to, and wind down the window to wave my schoolfellows goodbye.

Mrs Scott drove us off, passing through the town into country scenery. Our sleek bonnet nosed along a road overhung with dark trees, then, bursting again into sunlight, took us through a village at the far end of which was a duck pond. On the other side of the road was a small cricket field. A match was in progress. Mrs Scott halted the car on the grass verge closest to the ground. As the over ended and the field changed, a player taking his place in the deep kissed his hand to us in acknowledgment of the car's striking appearance.

'Isn't this just too wonderfully picture-postcardy,' Mrs Scott said. 'Look at those birds in the pond, mallards aren't they with those shiny heads?' She turned to me and asked some basic questions about how cricket was played. Then she put us into gear and we moved off once more. The Major, who had been fidgeting about next to me and had taken no part in the conversation now gave a little cough, a signal, it seemed, for Mrs Scott to slow down and pass over her shoulder a big tartan rug. 'Draughty, our old bus,' she remarked. 'You boys'll need this across your knees. We mustn't have you catching cold.'

The Major spread the rug over our laps, and made certain adjustments beneath its folds to ensure his personal comfort. Then I felt his signet ring on the flesh just above my right knee. I wondered from what metal it had been cast. Never had anything felt so cold. He coughed again and gave a quiet exclamation as if he had made an interesting discovery.

'Comfy at the back?' his wife asked.

'Very,' said the Major.

Like a nurse who, during a doctor's examination of a patient, pretends to busy herself with other affairs, Mrs Scott eased her driving seat forward an inch or two and pressed the car steadily ahead.

After a hotel tea, I rode back on the bus too full of food to have any appetite for the school supper of sausages and baked beans which we all voted to be the best meal of the week. I had a notion that a radical change had taken place within a routine rather treasured for being just that and to which, had I been thinking less wildly, it would have been sensible to revert. I was, though, obsessed with having another ride in the Scotts' motor-car at the earliest possible moment. An incident late in the day had dictated that my plan to astonish my friends by being collected in the Citroën now needed to be set against the likelihood next time I was asked out of making some money. When we'd garaged the car and had tea and I had said my goodbyes, the Major asked me how I planned to get back to school and how, for the matter of that, I had got to his hotel. When I told him it was on a local bus he took out his wallet, extracted a banknote and pressed it into my hand.

'Take this,' he said. 'We mustn't have you out of pocket. Come again soon and we'll kill another fatted calf. Ha.'

On the bus I calculated to the nearest penny, after subtracting my fare, the one pound forty I owed Ganson, and the estimated expenditure over the coming week at the school tuck shop, how much profit would be likely to accrue from the Major's five-pound note.

There had been some goings-on at the séance, Atkinson reported. Jayawickrama had perfectly grasped what was expected of him by putting to work the clairvoyant gift with which Wilkie Collins had written the eastern races were endowed. At least that was what was thought when the session began. He was urged to clear his mind of mundane thoughts and gaze into the ink pool in his hand as Rasputin had recommended and to let us know what he saw. He immediately claimed that he was 'in touch with a gentleman. He is Our Friend. He speaketh to me and telleth me to say unto you we are chosen from many to spread his message unto the world.' This was a piece of advice we felt uneasy at obeying, seeing that, in common with a good many grown-up occult cabals, we met in the strictest secrecy. It wasn't in any case at all the sort of thing we wanted to hear when compared with the earlier predictions Rasputin had presented, faulty though some of them had been, concerning school work, games, the mental instability of the teaching staff, tips likely to be in the post from elderly relatives, other, always practical, guidances. Jayawickrama was ordered to ask his communicant his name in case, as Amos suspected, a malignant entity had disconnected Rasputin from his earthly callers. Jayawickrama was unable to confirm to whom he had been talking. 'The gentleman is no longer in the room,' he said. 'He hath gone for a wee.'

To be fair to Jayawickrama, the most likely reason for this interpolation was that he had misinterpreted our endeavours as an exercise in extempore drama of an earthy, even kitchen-sink, school of thought when improvisation is used as a means of carrying the plot along and that in his report of Rasputin's brief absence he was merely temporizing while he thought up a way to push the action forward. This possibility was not considered by the group. Jayawickrama had been given his marching orders then and there. The afternoon had been written off as a complete waste of time.

In the course of the following week, Ganson, in a precocious exhibition of the proficiency in textual criticism that would lead him to a chair at Cambridge, had undertaken a closer reading of Collins's text than Amos had managed and informed us that the clairvoyant boy in *The Moonstone* wasn't Indian at all.

'Amos has got it all wrong,' he said. 'No wonder Rasputin was put out. The Indians in the book are all grown-up. Their medium is a little English beggar boy with fair hair who was living rough in the London slums. The Indians capture him and make him their vehicle for consulting the oracle. I know the very person. He isn't of course a beggar boy or he wouldn't be at St George's.'

Mucklestone was certainly no beggar boy to judge from expensive trainers from Oo May (my first acquaintance with the firm of outfitters about which there will be more to be told), a hooded top from the same manufacturer, white socks, and a pair of still whiter, sharply creased, tennis shorts. We explained that he had been selected because of his latent gift (which we would now awaken) for seeing into the future. He seemed pleased at being chosen and willingly agreed for some black ink to be poured into the hollow of his palm.

I was anxious to ask Rasputin which of three actions he would advise me to take with Major Scott: never to go near him again: to make only as many visits as it would take to persuade him to pick me up from school in his superb car, impress my friends, and then bail out: to keep myself in his good books, earn a lot more money for my travelling expenses and, in due course, be given the promised driving lessons. These thoughts preoccupied me to the extent that when it fell to me to pour out the ink into Mucklestone's palm I misjudged the quantity by a fair amount. The ink overflowed the boy's hand: escaped through his fingers: spattered over his white shorts: trickled down his bare legs. He looked down at the mess I had made of him and began silently to cry. He tried to wipe away his tears and succeeded only in smearing ink over his face. Then he started screaming. It took some while to shut him up, calm him down. Even then, it was clear he needed to be tidied up before we could ask him to have another go at the clairvoyance he had been commissioned to produce.

We agreed that our best plan would be to take off his shorts before the ink soaked through to his pants and to put him into the pair of the boilerman, Brill's, dungarees which were hanging on a hook on the Boot-Hole door. Within this strictly provisional covering – so he was assured – he could be surreptitiously bundled along the passage and into the showers while one of us got him some clean clothes from his bedside locker. Mucklestone's inbred fastidiousness, aired as we had observed by his immaculate turn-out on arrival, rebelled against being shovelled into the pair of demonstrably dirty, probably evil-smelling, workaday bib-and-braces in which no self-respecting member of the Mucklestone family, male or female, young or old, would ever have been seen alive or dead. Tears began again, turning to further shrieks of rage: disgust: despair at ever getting out of the room in one piece and correctly dressed, cries loud enough to be heard by anyone within earshot and fulfilling in a terrible way Jayawickrama's message from Rasputin, if Rasputin it was who had been on the line and not a mischievous elemental in disguise, that our creed should be trumpeted to the world at large.

The din alerted the prefect that afternoon on school patrol. The Boot-Hole door was thrown open. Havergal, head of his house, captain of cricket, prop forward, stood on the threshold. He switched on the light.

It had to be conceded that the scene meeting Havergal's gaze was, from a disciplinarian viewpoint, unsatisfactory on all levels. Here in this ill-lit cell blocking out an afternoon of glorious sunshine were four hulking louts of twelve and thirteen towering over the smallest and blondest seven-year-old in the school who had been heard screaming his head off, was partially unclothed, and smeared more or less all over by this time with jet-black ink. An interpretation could be formed, one that would take some explaining away, that an initiation ritual had been interrupted of a barbarous nature or an indecent one: possibly both.

Havergal asked what on earth we thought we were doing.

'An experiment in intergalactic psychokinesis which took an improbable turn. The situation, Havergal, is now under control.'

Amos spoke with authority. Havergal remained unsatisfied.

'What is that supposed to mean?'

'I should not have thought, Havergal, that I would have to explain the meaning, I will not add, the vital importance to everyone who has the future wellbeing of mankind at heart, of intergalactic psychokinesis. We're all agreed with that, aren't we, guys?'

Even Mucklestone, who may have fallen out with Havergal in the past over some infringement of rules and was looking for a chance to get his own back, gave a smile through his tears and nodded his head.

This was a clever move of Amos's, touching Havergal's only sensitive spot within an otherwise impenetrable carapace. Havergal's concern for saving the planet from ecological disaster by all means possible from recycling drink cans to tackling the recent threat of global warming by joining sit-ins in the holidays conflicted with an authoritarian stance on school matters. At these words, Havergal simmered down. It was not out of the question that he and Amos, on discovery of a mutual concern about the world's future, had discussed the question of the benefits of vegetarianism, most likely with reference to its voluntary, even compulsory, adoption as an antidote to disaster, thus forging a link between two personalities who could otherwise have been expected to clash over the less important matters, so Havergal had been persuaded, of school discipline.

'I didn't think anybody used bottled ink any more.'

Those were more or less Havergal's parting words. He gave permission for one of us to go to the junior dormitory, ordinarily out of bounds to all but its occupants, and fetch some clean clothes for Mucklestone on whom our subjugation of a senior boy had made a considerable impression; and dressed now in a pair of long trousers to hide his stained thighs, and with scrubbed face and hands he smilingly announced his willingness to proceed with whatever further manipulations of his mind and body that we had in mind.

'After that kerfuffle,' Amos said, 'we had better perform the Lesser Banishing Ritual of the Pentagram and then intone a mantrum.'

'Mantra,' Ganson said.

'That's the plural,' Amos said. 'Now, everybody ...'

We obediently got to our feet and vibrated the words of power that Amos had taught us, Yod He Vau He, Adonai, Eheieh, Agla, simultaneously turning to each of the earth's compass points and inscribing in the air the five-rayed star that Amos had specified. Then we seated ourselves in silence to await events. Some minutes passed. All at once, Mucklestone cried out: 'Look at Ganson. His brains are coming out of his ear.'

Thinking back on the incident, I recalled that Ganson had looked for some time as if he were asleep or, if not asleep then thrown back in his chair with his eyes shut. Now, as he lolled, apparently unconscious, what appeared at first to be a twist of cotton wool, though too big a twist to have been inserted into a comparatively small cavity, slowly discharged itself from Ganson's left ear, a grey curd of matter that ballooned outwards and altered its shape into three stemmed branches like the florets of a stale cauliflower. A few seconds later, its development ceased and the extrusion clung like a fungus, a faintly pulsating fungus, to the side of Ganson's neck. Then, as he moved and opened his eyes, whatever it was withdrew, disturbed perhaps by its host's arousal, back through the portal whence it had emerged. Ganson flinched as if this re-assimilation had caused him pain.

'Joke over, Ganson,' Akky said.

'What joke?' Ganson asked.

Afterwards, Amos warned us all to say nothing to anyone about the incident. 'What we saw was ectoplasm,' he said.

*

My research in the public library unearthed a book titled in translation *The Phenomena of Materialization*. It had been written by a German nobleman, a point I thought worth mentioning to Amos who gave as his opinion that high birth need not necessarily preclude nor, he warned, ratify, a qualification for serious psychical research. Accordingly, I must be watchful not to let the author's title dazzle my eyes. The book was lavishly illustrated with black-and-white flashlight photographs – *Blitzlichtaufnahmen* – the majority of which displayed incontrovertibly fraudulent behaviour on the part of the spiritualist mediums under investigation: mainly women of coarse appearance. Their favourite tricks were to brandish cardboard cut-outs of ghosts and to vomit up lengths of muslin they hoped the investigators would believe were constituted from the same ethereal stuff we had observed emerging from Ganson's ear. One photograph showed just such a ragged strip of material draped between the medium's breasts as if a net curtain had been loosely strung across a garret window. In the usual course of events, the book said, the dead spoke through metal trumpets provided by Baron Schrenk-Notzing and his fellow researchers. Some of these cone-shaped objects were illustrated floating about the room, allegedly apported by phantoms, although there seemed little doubt they had been tossed into the air by the fat perfidious women who had managed to loosen their arms from the ropes in which they had been bound. The photographs exemplified the tawdry, occasionally lubricious, atmosphere pervading the Baron's laboratory. Finding themselves tied up, in one case sewn into a sack, by men, always men, of higher rank than they, these women had responded by playing silly games. It seemed likely, given Amos's proviso about the unreliability of titled authors, that the Baron had gained as much satisfaction from bandaging these women to their chairs and watching their struggles as he had from witnessing the phenomena produced.

My fair knowledge of the German language, widened by Rasputin's exhortation to give it more attention, enabled me to translate the Baron's description of the intimate body searches he performed on his subjects before the séances got under way. These precautions were luridly described. Taken as a whole the pictures and the text of the book seemed to debase our Sunday enterprise and to depict a very different encounter between male and female parties of the type that, on occasion, was beginning to excite our curiosity but given a sadistic twist to which none of us had given so much as a thought. This was the position when, for the third or fourth time, I was invited to lunch with Major and Mrs Scott. With no advice forthcoming from Rasputin, I had opted for the course of accepting their every invitation so that I could make five pounds per visit, a sum that, when certain concessions were taken into account, could now be classed as earnings rather than profiteering. After lunch, we'd either all three go for a spin in the enviable car, or, if Mrs Scott had an appointment with her masseur, the Major and I would have a rest in his hotel room 'and let our lunch go down.'

On arrival, as often as not, I'd find Mrs Scott in the hotel lounge, engaged with the Sunday newspapers, coffee and a plate of chocolate biscuits in front of her. On the Sunday in question I had tucked the bulky Schrenk-Notzing under my arm not so much to read as to present the Scotts with an appearance of deep scholarly application. For once, Mrs Scott seemed unready for a chat. 'Sit down, dear. Have a coffee and a bikky. The Major will be down in a sec.' She licked her fingers, turned a leaf, tutted at what she read. I opened the Baron.

Just then, a member of staff came up and asked for Miss April Scrubbs. Mrs Scott nodded assent, rose, and followed the assistant out. I supposed Scrubbs must have been Mrs Scott's maiden name: further concluding she must be glad it could now be abandoned. I returned to the book. It appeared that the supposedly ectoplasmic extrusions the mediums produced could be transformed (by spirit hands) into a voice-box through which these beings could transmit their messages to the living. I was considering how best to pass this information on to Ganson who, since the occurrence, had hotly denied that he had been the vehicle for any abnormality and that the rest of us were winding him up, when Major Scott arrived.

'Deep in a book, eh? Looks very scholarly for a day off school. Geometry? Physics?'

I passed the Baron over. The Major thumbed through it, quickly at first, then slowing down. For a few minutes, he awarded it his closest attention, stopping every now and then to issue a grunt of disbelief at what he read, presuming he knew German, and the pictures before his eyes. Then he turned to me and said: 'This is filth.' He repeated the word, more loudly this time. A shower of spittle flew from between the buck teeth. He looked around him as if he wanted to alert everyone in the room to the revolting contents of the book he held in his hands and to bring shame on the creature – he was about to describe me as no more than that – who had ruined his Sunday by putting it in his hands. A few heads turned as he elaborated his comments, although in a slightly lower voice adjusted to match the intimate nature of a single aspect of the book's contents.

'This is disgusting, morbid nonsense. Look at this, look at this.' He jabbed a forefinger at one of the flashlight halftones that had caught his eye as an exemplar of especial horror. More spit rained over his misaligned teeth and landed on the photograph of a medium, tightly bandaged to her wooden chair. From between her legs a pallid rope of matter had been discharged. 'Look at that woman there. Filthy cheating bitch with a stinking fanny, making fools of good men and true. I never saw such a nasty piece of work. Dangerous too, and mad into the bargain, I shouldn't be at all surprised. And that is the way you'll go as well if you monkey with this horrible business. There can be no question about that. Your normal appetites will cease. You'll begin to waste away. People will discern a rancidness about you. You'll begin to give off an odour of decay, of foetor. Foetid: that's how you'll smell. Know what foetid means? Then, look...it...up.' He dropped the book into my lap and strode from the room.

That day Mrs Scott and I had lunch alone. Nothing occurred to lighten the gloom the Major had cast over the day except for a waiter who asked Mrs Scott, almost whispering his words, if he should serve her with 'a few beans', as though he were cautioning her not to overload her plate and so deprive other guests of their rightful helping. Ganson would laugh when I told him this. There was no outing in the car afterwards, no 'letting the lunch go down.' Mrs Scott did her best to soothe matters. 'I'd hop off now if I was you,' she said. 'I'm afraid the Major is having one of his goes. It may be his bad leg. It gives him gyp in this weather.'

I was badly shaken by what the Major had said. It was not at all out of the question that he would never want to see me again, that I had induced in him through my morbid hobby a repugnance at having me around, because, as he predicted, I already had warts on my face, sores on my legs, putrescent breath: foetid, as he had called it. To tell a young person he is diseased is hurtful enough: to warn him that he will become so sooner or later is worse by far because it initiates an anxiety that assails his every waking day, prompts him to examine himself in every mirror he can find, every shop window he passes, and in his cupped hands to test the quality of his exhaled breath for fear that the threatened blight has already taken hold.

It was a surprise to get a note from Mrs Scott asking me to come over the very next Sunday. I found the Major sitting at the table usually occupied by his wife. I was nervous that he had asked her to absent herself for a while so that he could continue last Sunday's harangue. He smiled up at me, putting on show the rabbit teeth.

'Ah, Leonard, Leonard, there you are, bang on time as usual. Good, good. Squattez-vous. Biscuits, biscuits, come along, dig in, there's a gap in the old tummy needs filling if I know anything about it, luncheon won't be for a while yet. We're promised apple pie again. That's good news, eh? With no custard. Naturally. I, ha, wanted a quick word in your ear before Mrs Scott puts in an appearance. I'm afraid I let my tongue run away with me last week. Truth to tell, I was frightened for your wellbeing. Boyhood is a very precious thing, you know. How I long for its return myself. That's not to be of course. There could well be another world where I shall become young again, I and everyone else. Who can tell and who can you blame you for exploring the chances we shall survive after we are dead, but reading a dirty German book won't give you any of the answers. Now, here's a little present that comes with my apologies for flying off the handle rather. I don't know whether you care for poetry but this fellow, he was Australian, wrote some rollicking lines you may care to look over and perhaps learn a few by heart. It's my hope it may go some way to smooth over any upset I may have caused.' That was when he handed me the collected poems of Adam Lindsay Gordon with the inscription Ganson had read out in the Jolly Herring:

> God who created me
> Nimble and light of limb,
> In three elements free,
> To run, to ride, to swim
> Take the thanks of a boy.

The Major read the lines aloud. 'That's all I meant when I rapped your knuckles about messing about with spiritualism. No lad of your age should hide himself in a darkened room when he can be out and about "in three elements free." Do you understand me? Now, I have had it in mind for some time to buy you a bicycle, but I'm not going to give a bicycle to a boy who's going to let it rust away in the bike sheds and sit about summoning spirits from the vasty deep. Ectoplasm, forsooth. There's only one form of ectoplasm a boy your age should be making, ha. Now, here comes Mrs Scott.' The Major showed his teeth again. He addressed his wife.

'My dear, I had been giving some thought to buying our young friend a bicycle. But it turns out he's been dabbling with things he shouldn't, ghoulies and ghosties and long-leggedy beasties, and things that go bump in the night. And boys like that don't need bicycles. Do you agree?'

Mrs Scott plumped down beside me and tapped me on the knee. Her bracelets rang out.

'Oh, you are a naughty boy. Scaring yourself half to death like that, it's no wonder you look a bit pasty. Don't you think he looks pasty, Thorold? A good lunch is what he needs and a blow in the car afterwards. That'll put the roses back in his cheeks. And then if he's good we might peep in the window of that bike shop in Peascod Street and see if there's anything that catches our fancy. What do you say to that?'

The gift of the bicycle heralded the very retrieval of clearheadedness the Major had called for, a state of mind at any age often to be brought about by hard exercise. I resigned from the spiritualist circle. I spent my free time pedalling about the countryside, reciting as I rode along the galloping verses of Adam Lindsay Gordon. Sometimes I was Dick Neville, the so-called amateur jockey in Gordon's poem about a steeplechase:

> A gentleman rider — well, I'm an outsider,
> But if he's a gent who the mischief's a jock ?
> You swells mostly blunder, Dick rides for the plunder,
> He rides, too, like thunder — he sits like a rock.

Sometimes I was astride the outsider who beat the favourite by a short head.

> The fourth fence, a wattle, floor'd Monk and Bluebottle;
> The Drag came to grief at the blackthorn and ditch,
> The rails toppled over Redoubt and Red Rover,
> The lane stopped Lycurgus and Leicestershire Witch.

> She passed like an arrow Kildare and Cock Sparrow,
> And Mantrap and Mermaid refused the stone wall;

And Giles on The Greyling came down at the paling,
And I was left sailing in front of them all.

After an hour or so in the saddle, I would I lie down and rest in a wheat field or under a tree where, like the young Anatole France in the Jardin des Plantes, I imagined that the sunbeams that pierced the leaves were the divine rays the Eternal Father allowed to escape from His fingers. I took up spin bowling again and the next year I was picked for the second eleven. My resignation heralded a general splintering of the table-turning group. Atkinson, also a keen cricketer, joined me in the school team. Ganson began to moon after girls. Only Amos continued to pursue paranormal enquiries. There had been some trouble in form, we heard, when a tract he had hidden beneath his school books was identified as a facsimile of an ancient textbook of black magic, the *Book of Goetia of Solomon the King*. Amos had marked with a cross three names from a long list of infernal spirits who, if the book's invocations were correctly pronounced, could be made his servitors in the pursuit of what had to be said, when Amos's ascetic cast of mind was taken into consideration, were decidedly worldly ambitions: *Haagenti* who has the ability to make men wise and turn all metals into gold; *Berith* (also known as *Bolfry*) who has the power to confer dignities and will give answers to all things past, present, and future; and *Sitri*, (he will appear with a leopard's head, Amos had noted, and the wings of an eagle), who enflames men with women's love and women with men's love and 'causes them to show themselves naked if it be desired.' Amos had underlined that passage. He had been in the act of tracing the sigils of these demons into an exercise book when the invigilating master had cut short his work. The grimoire was sent up to the headmaster who got in touch with Amos's parents.

I was barely fifteen when Major Scott began to give me driving lessons, taking me out to an old house with a carriage drive and putting me behind the wheel of his Citroën until I became modestly adept, although still too young to take my driving test. Then, I had a bad accident on the bicycle, breaking a leg. For a few weeks I was immobile. Soon after, I resumed my lessons until, one Sunday, just after my sixteenth birthday the Major asked me to ride over to the house instead of his driving me there. As we stood beside the car after my lesson he turned to me and held out his hand.

'Well done. You drive perfectly. If you can drive this old bus, you can drive anything. And now I must say goodbye.'

'Next Sunday then.'

'No, this is goodbye for ever.'

'Have I done something wrong?'

'Nothing.'

'I must have for you to be cross.'

'No, no. You haven't, but I insist that you go. Go, now. Don't come back. Remember me kindly as I shall remember you.'

I started to say something more, but he shouted at me angrily.

'I've told you: go! Go and get on with your life. I can't bear to look at you any more or listen to that croaking voice of yours. You are as good as dead to me now and I should be as good as dead to you.'

I biked back to school by a different route, one I had not explored before, a more roundabout way that might give me time to come to terms with my peremptory dismissal. It was a pointless exercise. I already knew for certain why I'd been ordered away. I was diseased. That was obvious. Major Scott wasn't in a bad temper just because his leg hurt him as it occasionally used to when he would sometimes cry off our lunch or the ride in the Citroën. It was I who was sickly, more than sickly: seriously ill. I was exhibiting the first signs of the decay, the physical 'foetor' with which the Major had threatened I would be leprously infected because of my dabblings in the unseen. He did not want me around him for fear he too would catch the disease. That could be the only reason for his shaking me off and shouting at me never to come near him again. I needed to find a mirror and examine my face to see how far the illness had advanced, already enough, it must be, for the Major to have recognised its telltale marks when we got out of his car into the sunshine of the afternoon. Mirrors at school were in short supply but there was one in the changing-room. Atkinson was there.

'Come out in the yard. Bring your bat.'

'Why?'

'I think I've perfected my wrong'un.'

'Not now.'

'Have you been crying? You look as though you've been crying.'

'I've got pinkeye.'

'Pinkeye's infectious.'

'Well, you'd better fuck off then.'

Akky feigned disgust. 'Oh, Eric that's the first time I ever heard you swear.'

He was quoting from a Victorian school story we had found in the library and whose pervasive sermonising we mockingly echoed.

' "Pooh, Edwin, you don't call that swearing, do you?" '

I managed Eric Williams's retort before, again, I burst into tears.

After a while anxieties eased. I no longer looked urgently in looking-glasses or tried my own breath. We often regard kindness with suspicion and question what is the true motive that has prompted the good samaritan to extend to us his hand. So far as the Scotts were concerned, I reasoned I must have been taken up because they had no son of their own, a son in name only, a boy whose age and circumstances absolved the two would-be parents from full-time care and who would divert them only at prearranged intervals convenient to themselves, someone, then, not much more than a plaything. To circumvent any such suspicion that that was the role he had been called upon to play, this person must be fed with hotel meals, presented with a racing bicycle, paid money, bribed, – one could go so far – to act out the filial role he had been recruited to fill. Deception had been on all sides, the Major's for incidents not to be categorised as fatherly despite his condoning and for the matter of that, imitating the maternal disposition of his wife whose outbreaks of affection when, quite often, she would clasp me to her flowered bosom or chuck me under the chin seemed genuine manifestations of a frustrated motherliness, mine for keeping the two of them on a string in order to tuck into their food, ride about in their Citroën, then to sit behind its wheel, and to pocket a commission for 'services rendered.' The only things I genuinely missed, in a way Major Scott might well have interpreted as evincing the frank and boyish spirit he held should be an essential part of my makeup, were the Sunday lunches and the five-pound-notes.

CHAPTER III

'Wotcha, Drain'ole.'

This was Terence's invariable greeting whenever I visited the in-laws resident in a seaside town where Terence had for many years run an electrical business. The story went that Molly had taken in some gadget or other in need of repair and had fallen in love with the man behind the counter in no respect at first sight to have been accounted her social equal. That turned out wrong. Terence's self-consciously Cockney salute as much as the brown overall he was wearing when Molly's heart was stirred in her bosom disguised an upbringing much the same as his wife's. Terence Davidson was the son of a clergyman, Molly Pash a solicitor's daughter. For all that, a rude exterior suited Terence both in furtherance of his trade and in dealing with Molly, at times inclined in his words to 'be all kippers and curtains.' 'Drain'ole' was his interpretation of my Christian name pronounced backwards.

On the drive up, one passed through a small town where an infinitely protracted roadworks would halt the car outside a spiritualist church. The building offered no architectural feature to be associated with places of worship – steeple, stained glass, porch, buttressed walls, outlying churchyard – other than a carved gothic notice-board above which a golden roundel had been affixed incorporating the words LIGHT TRUTH NATURE. A dove, probably representing a departed person returning briefly to earth in convenient form and bringing comfort to the living with news of a happier and, to judge from the whiteness of the bird's plumage, a purer world beyond the veil of un- knowing, swooped downwards across this enigmatic lettering. As well as Sunday service times, the board advertised weekday events scheduled within this lowly pile, a development circle, clairvoyance readings, spiritual healing, coffee mornings. Once, I had time to remark that beneath a thin coat of paint the words 'Hester Dowden Memorial Hall' remained legible in the bright sunlight. Hester, long dead, the daughter of old Edward Dowden, Goethe enthusiast, poet, critic, had become a medium, publishing books retailing her conversations with famous men in the spirit world. Oscar Wilde and Francis Bacon had been two of those who had got in touch. Her father had most likely disapproved of his daughter's truck with the demised, his own verse displaying a measure of doubt concerning an afterlife.

The forlorn nature of this church's exterior may not necessarily have reflected the decline of the spiritualist movement, buffeted since its foundation by persistent accusations of fraudulent practice by critics sometimes as noisily antipathetic as Major Scott had been on examining my copy of *Materialisations-Phaenomene* thirty or so years ago but have been deliberately maintained by the faithful as a symbol that in the meanest surroundings the dead are by our side. It was odd that such a creed maintained some sort of a foothold when others of that era, New Lifers, Flat Earthers, British Israelites, phrenologists, had been consigne to the scrap-heap. My mother-in-law's cousin, Yseult, sometimes visiting the Davidsons at the same time as I, professed allegiance to a similar long-forgotten creed, although discouraging spiritistic intercourse as 'glamorous'. Despite having given up my schoolboy dabblings, I was still not an absolute disbeliever in psychic phenomena, whether it was the dead who 'came through', as affirmed by the faithful of the church where I was held up, or not. I thought not, simply because of the banality of their reports from the Other Side. Yseult agreed. 'Body, soul, spirit, those are the three steps,' she said, adding that spiritualistic manifestations were caused by spiteful elementals having nothing much better to do with their time.

For a short period after Ann's death I had been tempted to return to these arcane practices, going so far one day as to park the car and try the door of the church, luckily for me found locked and bolted. The chance that I might be able to communicate with my wife if I could find a medium who could bring about her manifestation had not helped me recover as fast as I should otherwise have done from my period of incarceration under Dr du Sautoy who, in common with Major Scott, saw my preoccupation as morbid in the extreme. It was fortunate that I did not have charge of my son at such a critical time. The in-laws were bringing George up, brought him up even now, the reason for my more or less regular trips to where they lived.

After my recovery and my acceptance of Ganson's offer as a teacher in his Academy, practical difficulties had forbidden, or, rather, I made out that they had forbidden, George's coming to live with me. This was not an ideal state of affairs so far as his grandparents were concerned. Even with their own child, Terence and Molly had not had much idea how to go about things. They had realised at once, 'from my first scream,' Ann used to say, that what they really wanted was a grown-up near-relation of about twenty years old, who, in due course would present them with a grandchild over whom they could coo on days when it suited them. Terence kept his daughter at a distance. He would have felt less awkward had Ann been a boy able to help him in his business and later on take it over. Molly gave the impression of being put out, of being unable to cope with a role preferably to be left to a nanny or to a nursemaid if one had been within her means. Neither parent had been in the least unkind. Ann described them as merely bewildered by what they had brought into the world: enormously relieved when their daughter got married. When she died and they were obliged to bring up George because of my state of mind they found they were back where they started and none the wiser for its being the second time around. George had failed to revive what in the first place had been no more than an atavistic requirement. Once when Molly had insisted on George's wearing a suit I had heard her exclaim, 'You look very grown-up' as if she saw in the small uncomfortable figure the grown man for whom she would no longer have to bear responsibility.

In addition to their child-rearing necessities, the convention of the Davidsons' marriage had turned out unsatisfactorily, or so I thought. Molly often said she had married 'rather a juggins.' That seemed a harsh estimate of Terence's intellect, which, despite Molly's judgement, could never be measured at any great height on the 'juggins' spectrum. His head for business had not tampered with his sportive nature – the feature his wife may have taken for silliness. For example, well into his sixties he played bass guitar with a local ensemble called the Otiose Umlauts ('the "lauts" bit made us sound as if we were punks, but we weren't'), a band founded as a tribute to a successful American group to which I too had been rather addicted, although at an age when Molly felt able to allow a youthful ingenuousness to prevail over her own maturer taste, as she saw it, for classical music.

'She only likes Chopin,' Terence said. 'I tell her she ought to "Shop A-round" for some other music to listen to.'

He paused for my appreciation of the joke. Like all punsters, he needed handling with the utmost severity. Early on in our acquaintance, a simple solution presented itself. I would pretend not to have grasped the word-play, continuing the conversation as if nothing had happened. This might have been thought to upset Terence. It had the opposite effect, setting him off in a burst of laughter at one's fraudulent obtuseness. This jocularity with words, verging at times upon juggins-ism, had inspired Terence to write three books for children, illustrated by one of his old band-mates and published, coincidentally, by the same small publisher issuing the poetry of O. G. Ganson. One of Terence's titles, *The Revolting Mrs Boulting*, had been banned from a provincial university library, I think Sussex's, for belittling womankind. For that reason it had outsold the other two. There was talk of an animated cartoon version. In the way that the descendants of authors do not, by and large, warm to their families' books, George did not favour his grandfather's, complaining that the words used by Mrs Boulting were too long and the various predicaments involving Mrs Boulting and her friend, the Embarrassin' Mrs Harrison, unconvincing in the extreme.

I looked forward to my visits, sometimes to have expectations dashed soon after arrival. There was occasionally some awkwardness that made me regret my coming. The in-laws could bicker, creating what George called an 'atom-o-sphere.' Once when I got there, he was wearing a smart yellow hooded top. Across the front were embroidered the letters, 'Oo May.'

'He wears that when he goes out with the girls,' Terence said. 'It's short for "Oo, may I give you a smacking kiss".'

'As a matter of fact, grand-dad, it's two Greek words put into English. ' "Never ever." '

' "Never, ever have I looked so frightful." '

George was not to be roused.

' "Never better," actually.'

Molly looked up from a book she was reading. 'Declare me if there's isn't a page missing.'

'No, there's not,' Terence said.

'I'm saying there is.'

'There isn't.'

'I tell you, there is.'

'There can't be. It is a scientific impossibility. A page couldn't be missing. It could be blank, it could be misprinted, it could be mis-aligned, smudged with ink, spat upon, covered in gravy, but it couldn't just be missing.'

'Well, look then.'

Terence took the book then handed it back.

'Just as I said. A page isn't missing. A leaf is missing.'

'Well, whether there is or whether there isn't, there's no call for rudeness. Rude is never funny, I always say.'

'Always, darling? Don't you bore yourself to death?'

Looking back on it, my son's loyalty was astounding. He had every right to disown me as any kind of a father. Indeed, when he was very small that was what he appeared to be doing. He would look at me with a stare of incomprehension as if he failed completely to understand why this man whom so far as he knew he had never seen before and never wanted to see again should believe for one moment that by saying hello and waving his arms about in what he must suppose was a comical fashion could gain his attention for one single second. When he was about ten, that all changed. He would hurl himself at me when I turned up and hug me round the waist, a signal for me to raise my arms above my head in an attitude of surrender to this impulsive affection. Seats had to be found for us there and then before any refreshment was offered or I had time to greet his grandparents. News tumbled from him. He'd been to a school camp, there had been a ghost walk, it was so scary two boys had had accidents if I knew what he meant, he liked cricket more than football, in fact it would be fair to say he didn't like football at all very much, he had got nineteen out of twenty in his maths test although maths was boring and he liked English best. Names of his friends were fired off, boys, never girls, I had never set eyes on, as if I were well acquainted with them all and about whom I would be bound sooner or later to enquire so that it would be better for me to be brought up to date straight away with their latest exploits, Dylan, Arlo, Emil, Reuben: their achievements in school and on the playing field in his opinion ranking well below his own.

'I'm glad you're making friends.'

He stared at me incredulously as if I hadn't grasped one word of what he'd been talking about.

As he had grown, some of his ideas – 'fads,' to Molly's way of thinking – had much to commend them. He had a theory that food tasted unpleasantly odd if eaten with a different implement from the conventional one and had once refused to eat baked beans when they were served up in a bowl with a spoon. 'It will make them taste like pudding,' he said as he pushed the food aside. It is often said that boys are greedy creatures but in George's case this was not true. He ate sparingly and thoughtfully, sometimes collapsing limply in his chair as if drugged by what he had been foolish enough to put in his mouth. Then he would slide slowly downwards in his seat until he vanished from sight. The rest of the mealtime would be spent under the table. To amuse him in his retreat, he took with him a tablet on which he played an endless game of warfare. Every so often under the cloth gun-fire could be heard as inhuman creatures, or so I assumed, did each other in. When, as often happened, the gadget had been confiscated, he seemed just as happy to crouch silently in his underground bothy where valuable information could be gleaned from a laddered stocking, unmatching socks, the entwining of legs, and a deep contentment that he was generating nervousness among the more formal of his grand-parents' guests at receiving a tweak on the calf or a bite on an ankle.

There would come a time in his day, not necessarily towards its close, when, after I had believed I was communicating with a person of a certain level of intelligence, he would jettison a dimension of his existence, perhaps the etheric double believed by Molly's cousin, Yseult, to be part and parcel of our embodiment, and devolve into an apathetic state of mind that denied response to any kind of approach. I found this extremely annoying and rather rude especially on a day that had been spent on some treat or other, until I came to understand that it was a symptom of exhaustion. George was tired out. One minute he'd be whizzing about all over the place, the next huddled in a chair, resistant to any social approach, curling his dark brown hair through his fingers and wiping his hands across his face as if his skin were covered with the adhesive filaments of a spider's web.

If we were not going out anywhere, he was anxious for us to sit down together so that he might impart shards of knowledge it was impor-tant for me to grasp in case my ignorance of them, that came about because of my getting on a bit and consequently not fully conversant with modern developments, might land me in difficulties of one sort or another when he was not by my side to offer assistance. Informa-tion poured from him: car registration numbers, the square root of two, molecule structure, electrical circuiting, anatomical details with espe-cial reference to the intestinal tract, books I must read, 'chapter' books he called them to indicate they were on the grown-up side and didn't have pictures in them, riddles to which I never knew the answers. This bombardment needed to be curbed as being too indigestible for an aging mind and, one day, in order to shut him up for a minute,

I performed a vanishing trick with a pound coin. I'd shown him it once before when he was much younger. Then it had fallen flat. To small children things vanish inexplicably all the time. For us to make them do so is nothing but a repetition of a daily and tiresome occurrence in a child's life. 'Ball: gone' was a constant lament when George had been five or six. Now, at ten years old, not only did he love the trick and demand to be taught it but, because at its climax I had said the magical word 'Abracadabra' (unoriginal but one-up on Terence's 'Lo Plus Behold') he adapted the word for his own use, employing it when he hit a cricket ball to the fence that acted as a boundary in the garden or when he had polished off the cake on his plate. I took his hand to show him the move necessary to perform the vanish, at the same time swearing him to secrecy. Magicians, I told him, are jealous guardians of their secrets. He must never, ever, give away any of his secrets.

'How come you are so good at magic?'

'I learned as a boy: much your age. Anyway, it's in our blood. The Saunders's are descended from a family of popular entertainers, circus artists. One of our ancestors was a tight-rope walker.'

'What's that?'

'Someone who balances on a rope stretched between two poles, high up in the air. People use a wire these days.'

George quickly added tightrope-walking to his battery of knowledge, asking for the names of the most prestigious performers throughout the ages and at what height from the ground they performed their acts. 'Don't encourage him, Leonard,' Molly said. 'We don't want a tightrope in the garden, not with the trampolines and slateboards and scooters and all the other bits and bobs. There'd be broken legs and I don't know what else besides. We'll stick to cricket, thank you. That's dangerous enough in all conscience, now he insists on playing with a hard ball. I blame that Cyrus boy.'

Behind his grandmother's back, George raised his eyebrows at me.

I'd heard Cyrus spoken of before. 'Tall for his age' Molly had said. This was to be taken as a sign of her disapproval of some aspect of George's friend's behaviour when under her roof and not as an estimation of his stature compared with her grandson's or other boys she knew or had known in the past. I wondered why Molly disapproved of him. Perhaps it was simply that his height allowed him to bowl faster and to hit cricket balls harder than was consistent with safety in the back garden.

'Who is Cyrus?'

'My best friend at school. His father is very rich. Who was the most famous tightrope walker in all history?'

On George's eleventh birthday, and what would turn out to be nearly my last visit, I was as usual ordered to sit down. George settled himself beside me. 'Hello, dad.'

'Hello.'

'Guess what.'

'What?'

'On Thursday, I was sick in Prewett's.'

George looked at me steadily when he said that as if I must now solicit from him some more details of a piece of news that, if allowed elaboration, would prove of gripping moment. Molly did her best to forestall any further specifics of the matter in whatever category.

'I'm sure Daddy doesn't want to hear any more about that little incident.'

In order to please both parties – or at least not to upset Molly at such an early stage of my visit – I asked only who Prewett was.

'A shop,' George said. 'I wasn't sick in it much. Then I went outside and was sick some more on the pavement. Quite a lot more, basically. It's been cleared up now. I wonder who did that.'

'There are sick scourers in this town,' I said. 'Employed by the council. They are on duty day and night, three hundred and sixty-five days a year, twenty-four seven as you would say. No pool of vomit is countenanced to remain on their territory for more than half-an-hour after it has been deposited. Otherwise, these men are relieved of their position. Jailed sometimes.'

'You're fibbing,' George said.

'I'm fibbing a bit.'

'You're fibbing lots.'

Molly got up. 'If you two are going to be disgusting,' she said, 'I'll have my coffee somewhere else.'

Now we had been left on our own, wide vistas were open to discussion: the reactions of Mr Prewett to George's mishap, possibility of a barring-out in perpetuity from his place of business, the upset stomach a result of the goods on offer, the colour and constituents of the voided substances. Questions were enthusiastically answered. A bond had been created. Then Terence came in. It needed saying that these days he was not as mentally alert as he once had been. He was often to be found sitting in a chair, staring into space, and every now and then announcing the time of day in the manner of a speaking clock. He did it again.

'It's gone the half-hour, boys.'

'Is there anything we should be doing?' I asked.

Terence made no reply. I turned to George with some question or other. He didn't answer either. I asked him again. He made no reply. I tried a third time.

He looked up frowningly as if he had heard something or other, although certainly not the voice of his father, not even a human voice, but an alien sound, the miaow of a cat or the leathery flap of a bat's wings as it flew above his head, a sound odd enough to have roused him from a coma of unplumbable depth. As time went by, I learned to ignore these torpid periods which were not to be interpreted as surliness or lack of enthusiasm for what was on offer but as a temporary uncoupling of a part, a not unenviable part, of childhood – or boyhood at least – associated perhaps with mental development that allowed him time to master a complex engine of which for the moment he had not completely grasped the mechanics. I suggested we go out for a walk.

When he was younger and we'd gone out, I'd always worried that he might get lost along the way because, in the manner of a dog, he would run off ahead of me, sniffing out a trail for his master to follow. On this occasion, he marched along at my side. His untied shoelaces slithered like dutiful kraits in his path.

'Grandpa's always announcing what time it is,' he said. 'For no reason that I can see. I think he may be on the verge of a nervous bread van.'

'He's getting old.'

'He must have had mum very late.'

'He did.'

'I wish she was still here.'

George turned his head away. He was crying. Then he wiped the back of his hand across his eyes.

'Sorry to cry, dad.'

'There's no need to be sorry.'

'There is. It's always a happy day when you come.'

For the first time in his life and mine, I put my arm around him. 'Let's buy some sweets. But not in Prewett's.'

'Thanks, dad,' George said when we came out of the shop. He pressed into my hand a piece of paper that I took to be an urgent billet containing information too sensitive to read out loud. It was a toffee-paper. George never carried anything if he could possibly help it, loading up his grandparents with his school bag, cricket pads, jerseys, whatever accoutrements he had decided would be needed in what he had conceived to be an expedition likely to last all day, possibly all night, long.

'I am your father, George, not your servant.

> The brisk fond lackey to fetch and carry,
> The true, sick-hearted slave.

He looked up at me blankly and handed me another sweet-wrapping. Later, on the pier we bought ice-creams. George smiled up at me through clown's lips.

'Can I borrow a pound coin?'

'For another ice cream? We don't want a repercussion of the Prewett incident.'

'No, just for something. Look.'

He vanished the coin perfectly. The move was not difficult but it needed careful timing to make the disappearance look effective.

'Abracadabra.'

'Abracadabra, indeed. You've been practising.'

'Yes, ever since you were last here. Grand-dad lent me his video camera so's I could film myself in action.'

For the next hour we talked magic. He was keen for me to buy him a box of tricks, a 'magic set' he called it, that he had seen in a shop. We could go there now. There was time before tea. The selection of tricks in the box turned out boring: the same effects I had learned when I was a boy, age-old even then: the ball in the vase, the cricket bat with a jumping matchstick, a few patently faked playing cards, a magic wand which did nothing and was just a black stick with white ends, a thumb-tip that would have been too big for George's hand. I persuaded him to settle instead for a pack of cards which, more or less self-working, provided several different ways of revealing a spectator's choice. The final and most startling discovery was made by wrapping the entire pack in a paper napkin and stabbing the parcel with a table-knife that disclosed underneath its blade the freely chosen card.

As we walked home we passed a litter-bin marked 'General litter.'

George stopped by it. He raised his hand and touched his forehead in a military salute.

'My name is General Litter. I am head of the army. We are going to attack.' Terence must have put him up to this.

'I must contradict you, sir. My name is General Waste and it is I who am head of the army, not you. We are going to retreat.'

By the time we got back to the in-laws, we had conscripted a fair-sized military detachment, with three Generals, Waste, Litter, and Bloody-mindedness; Major Works; Corporal Punishment; and Privates Enterprise, Road, Parts, and Banking. George added Private Means.

'It's what grand-dad says you've got,' he said.

'Got what?'

'He says you've got private means. Otherwise you wouldn't be able to afford my school fees.'

I changed the subject. Even twenty years after what now could be put down as a windfall continued every so often to prick a conscience temporarily laid to rest by the passing of time. I hadn't long left school, certainly it was before I went to university, when I embarked on an affair in which my lover suggested a trip to a spa town in the west of England. She recommended a grand hotel. I was left to my own devices while Sylvia bathed in sulphuric waters and wallowed in mud baths. These disciplines combatted possible weight increase from heavy meals in the hotel restaurant and a fair amount to drink at its bar. Reclining one morning in a communal pool of healing salts, she had struck up a conversation with her masseuse, a tall thin girl, a wizard at breaking up the crystals that form at the back of the neck, Sylvia reported. The masseuse also did some modelling. Her hotel job was only temporary, it seemed. She was about to fly to the Gulf States on an important photo-shoot. Years later, bumping into Sylvia at a university reunion, I learned she had died.

Melissa began to join us in our evenings together, without offering to pay for her share of the expensive wines Sylvia chose from the hotel's list. Further outlays, which to be fair were not put on my bill, were incurred by the women's mutual enjoyment of cocaine. Another indulgence may have existed from which I was necessarily excluded. I was never sure on that point. I gave Sylvia twenty-four hours' notice that I was checking out. She shrugged her shoulders and returned to her immersions. I became increasingly anxious that I would not have the money to settle the hotel bill so I called in at the local branch of my bank to find out exactly how much money I had in my account. A cashier, advised not to confirm verbally the current balance, if any, that stood to a customer's name but allowing our eyes to meet in a moment of collaboration, wrote something on a piece of paper and passed the folded note across the counter. It could have read 'minus £71.48' or 'How about meeting in the next door wine bar, five-thirty sharp?' Her expression suggested either message to be on the cards. The paper showed a credit balance of £49,878.53.

This of course was impossible. Once when Molly had been overdrawn at her bank, Terence told me, she had complained to the manager who had called her into his office, 'Your men must have made a mistake.' A mistake had been made here, that was for certain: a mistake of mammoth proportions. It gave me breathing space, though. I could pay off the hotel and give myself a bit of time to rake up enough money to cover the debt before the error was noticed and the fifty thousand-odd pounds taken back. As it turned out, that was unnecessary. For six or seven years until I was married and George was born and cash had become more of a prerogative I had of course been prepared to return the money when asked for it as I surely would be sooner or later but as time went by and no such demand was received I had invested it in an old warehouse, thinking to open a sports academy. Come the nineties with the rise of online shopping, a big mail-order firm made me a decent offer for the building. I was advised not to sell outright but to rent it out. The income was considerable, enough to pay for George's schooling and to absolve me from having to earn a living. I resisted this dispensation, telling myself I could not possibly sit around doing nothing all day long, so, when I came out of hospital, I took on the teaching job at Ganson's academy: for some suppressive reason never letting my employer know of my modest wealth nor its original source. The nearest I got to telling anyone about this stroke of fortune was a short conversation I had with a fellow-undergraduate. I asked him what he would do if he suddenly found his bank account had been credited with fifty thousand pounds. His reply was, 'Nothing. I'd keep quiet and hope the mistake was never noticed. Were you the lucky man?'

'No, a friend.'

'What did he do?'

'He followed your advice.'

'And became rich.'

'Yes.'

Back home, George tried the card trick on Molly. Child conjurors are seldom given a fair chance in front of their equals who know quite well their friend is not possessed of magical powers. They are served far worse by grown-ups who either patronise them, fail to obey their instructions or award them with the close attention their mysteries deserve. Molly exhibited these deficiencies in quick succession. 'Go and wash your hands, George. I'm not going to play cards with a boy with dirty hands,' she said. She turned to Terence, 'Do you remember when we had those canasta evenings with the Dill-Russells? I could never quite get my head round the rules.' When George came back smelling of soap and she was eventually persuaded to take a card over Terence's observation that in the days of the Protectorate playing-cards were called the devil's picture book, she first of all forgot the value of the card she had chosen so that when George magically produced it she denied he had picked the right one. Then, after she had admitted she might have made a mistake, the effect went on well enough for a while so that with the second revelation of her card she allowed herself a little 'ooh' of surprise. She then objected to the use of the kitchen knife recommended in the trick's instructions for the final and most sensational of all the discoveries when, blindfolded with his grandmother's scarf (a clever finesse of George's), he asked her to hold the wrapped pack against his dagger thrust.

'I don't think we want to mess about with knives, do we?' Molly said. She turned to Terence and me for confirmation.

I was wondering,' George said as the trick was abandoned in deference to his grandmother's nervousness, 'when we come down and see you next if I could stay on after the grands go back and maybe Cyrus could come as well. He's older than me, so basically he could look after me while you're at work.'

The suggestion that George should come and stay was one of many his grandparents had raised on and off over the years as a way of temporarily unloading their responsibilities and one which I had always rejected as unfeasible, giving in excuse that my duties at the Academy would mean I'd have to leave him alone in the flat for most of the day or farm him out somewhere in working hours or hire a babysitter, a design, as I further protested, he would reject as an indignity. The fact was that an extended visit by George or anybody at all for the matter of that would be an intrusion into a life where solitude was more or less sacrosanct. These days, though, my attitude towards my son was changing. I was much more at ease with him now we had forged our conjuring link and his request to spend some time at my place suggested he felt the same way about me. I tentatively agreed.

'I suppose so. Where will you both sleep, though?'

'I thought perhaps we could have your big bed …'

'… And I could sleep on the put-you-up?'

'That's the sort of thing.'

Molly looked up from her paper. 'You'll be making,' she opined as she licked a finger, 'a rod for your own back.'

On the contrary. It turned out an excellent plan. I had expected a lot of noise and mess, excessive appetites followed by stomach aches, perhaps an outbreak of an infectious disease that would postpone the boys' departure by several weeks. I was called on for very little. Cyrus, 'tall for his age' as Molly had disparagingly described him as if extra height disposed him to extra wickednesses, was a charming guest. He and George amused themselves, got their own meals without making a mess in the kitchen or ate on their own in the downstairs café. Cyrus was a cricket enthusiast which meant I was, for once, not called on to face George's bowling in the village nets. I told Cyrus how well I thought he behaved.

'Boys are a maligned species,' he said.

There was only one accident while the two were with me. We were watching television when our lights fused.

'Leave it to me,' George said.

'Don't you think we should get an electrician?'

'Let him fix it, sir,' Cyrus said. He insisted on calling me Sir despite my protests. 'He is a master of his craft.'

When George was out of the room, Cyrus said, 'Sir, why doesn't George live here? He wants to but I said I thought it was perhaps you might not be able to afford it. If that's not being impertinent.'

'It's not that I'm not rich enough. It's that I'm not good enough: as a father.'

'Oh but you are. You're heaps better than my dad who to tell you the truth is rather a shit.'

Cyrus proved to be right about George. Whatever he did to the fuses took only ten minutes. Lights were restored. George returned.

'I said "shit" in front of your father.' Cyrus bowed his blond head.

George was unimpressed. 'Go figure,' he said. He climbed onto my lap. He had never done that before. I congratulated him on his handiwork. He threw back his head to smile at me upside-down. George was sparing with his smiles. That is not to say he was a glum boy or a sulky one or an unhappy one, simply that he reserved smiling for those occasions that warranted a display of genuine pleasure. He had a small gap between his two front teeth. I traced it with my little finger.

'That's my whistling gap,' he said. 'Listen.'

'I could never do that. I could only whistle through my lips: this way. Can you do the hooting owl thing? With your hands together. Like so.'

'No. Cyrus can.'

'I could never sit on my dad's lap,' Cyrus said. 'He'd throw me off. Like he does the cat. Can we have the television back on?'

'Of course.'

George observed the screen with his head on one side. He passed his fingers over his eyes, a sign, as I had come to understand, that he was tired. On the television, a man ran towards a car: climbed in: started the engine. The car blew up. Smoke and flames filled the screen.

'No more curried eggs for him,' Cyrus said.

It marks me as unfeeling to say that only at that moment, after twelve years of his life, did George insinuate his way into my affections. 'Insinuate' in any case is to accuse him of being somehow underhand, of plotting a seduction by playing on the fact that I was his father and that it was high time I did something about it. Now, on this night, he had sealed this bond by his very existence that I had finally come to comprehend as an existence of infinite preciousness, to the secure furtherance of which it was my duty and mine alone to guarantee. It came to me as George settled against me that here was love, love at its simplest. No bed, no jealousies, no drink, no drugs, no rivals. I loved my son, loved every facet of his nature and every moment of his presence. Even the clothes he was wearing resolved themselves into objects of infinite preciousness and of pathos, like the reliquary cloths that have cooled the brows of saints. His skin had a texture unlike any other texture I had ever touched and the aroma exuding from his brown hair that by rights should have smelled of the pizza which we had had for supper and of the crisps which he and Cyrus had been attacking as they watched the terrible film on television, exuded a sweetness like woodland earth, after rain.

George had become heavier, his breathing soft, measured. My son was asleep in my arms.

For me, that night, there was no sleep. Sleep was impossible on the wave of an emotion every bit as powerful as – and categorically different from – the one when I was head over heels in love with Ann. A fundamentally dull life had been illuminated by the peeling away of the cataracts of disillusionment with which my eyes had been clouded since her death, the revelation coinciding with the exploding motor-car in the televised thriller I had been watching with the boys. Happiness was mine again, true happiness what's more, for I gave no thought to its being that. No-one is ever truly happy if the mood needs propping up with its consideration. Any mood, for the matter of that, pales once it is categorised as such. This abandonment was tempered only by a schedule of work needing to be done in a very short time, by the morning in fact, letters to be written, emails to be sent, to the in-laws, to George's school, to Ganson requesting a leave of absence from the Academy, to the solicitor who handled the lease of the flat, to the garage. I made coffee, fired off texts, drew diagrams on the computer screen demonstrating how furniture could be shuffled round to accommodate an extra person. I had sent Cyrus off to bed and had slipped off the sofa without disturbing George. I resisted lighting cigarettes in a room that was sweet with his sleeping breath.

Early in the morning, I thought I might tackle the box-room. It was situated under the eaves, accessible only through a trapdoor set into the ceiling above the middle of the staircase. It would make a perfect bedroom for George. A stepladder would be needed to get up there. I'd borrow one from the café when it opened at eight. I was wondering whether someone could construct a more permanent access to this attic area when I heard a noise from the landing above.

Cyrus was looking down on me.

'There's nothing really special up there, sir,' he said. 'Only heaps and heaps of old books which, if you liked, I could help you bring down.'

Cyrus wore a white nightshirt or more likely an elongated singlet, one of exemplary cleanliness. In his right hand he held an unsheathed sword. His bare feet and the shimmering tunic he wore, his armed hand, his golden hair, his sudden and silent manifestation, proposed the visitation of a ministering angel, kindly but firm – retributive capacities in no manner to be underestimated – descended to help me with my task of preparing the house for the reception of my son.

> Who sweeps a room as for Thy laws,
> Makes that and the action fine.

That seemed the exhortatory message Cyrus was delivering.

'Perhaps I shouldn't tell you this,' he said, 'but George said it'd be a super place for him to live in, hint, hint. He reckons it would make a cool ...'

'... space capsule, smuggler's cave, bandits' lair, scriptorium, bolt-hole, yes, I know, that's my idea too. I'm going to have him to live here permanently, just as you told me I should. Only, please don't tell him. I want to do that myself. How do you know there are books up there?'

The boys had explored the box-room, Cyrus said. Some discoveries had been made, the old books unearthed. The sword had been found there. Cyrus had polished it up.

'There's an extension ladder next to the trapdoor,' Cyrus said, 'that lets down onto the stairs. I could get up on your shoulders if you liked and slide it down to you. Perhaps I oughtn't to, though, now I come to think about it.'

'One of us could fall down the stairs. Or both together.'

'I didn't quite mean that.' Cyrus offered a smile, breaking for the first time the mould of a celestial being seldom given to humour and journeyed down at a time not especially convenient time to itself to administer reproof to a soul thought to have gone astray.

'What did you mean?'

'Well, you see, I haven't put my pants on yet.'

'That could be dangerous in the extreme,' I said.

'It could, couldn't it.' Cyrus's smile broadened as he said that.

•

Next day, Cyrus was collected in a bright red car with a pugnacious bonnet matching to some degree the distended belly of a father who pushed his son into the back seat, then violently took my hand. Cyrus's appraisal of his parent's basic nature was instantly ratified.

'Kind of you to have had the sprog. Hope he behaved himself.' Cyrus senior proffered some banknotes retrieved from a pocket in a pair of khaki shorts, tenuously supported. I shook my head. We waved goodbye.

'Red car, small cock,' George observed.

'That seems a fair corollary.' I put my arm around George's shoulders. 'Would you like to come and live here?'

'For how long?'

'For ever and ever.'

'Do you really mean it?'

'Of course.'

'Oh, dad.'

'So then, the next time you come, it will be for good.'

'Can I just stay now and not go back?'

'Why, aren't you happy with the grands?'

'They're all right. Sort of. Grand-dad's getting a bit weird. He keeps telling us what the time is although we haven't asked and don't care. And gran, well, she's just gran. She says grand-dad's got dementia peacocks. But really, it's just, you see, if I did go back, you might change your mind after I'm gone.'

CHAPTER IV

Some difficulties had to be got over. George would sometimes have to be left alone in the flat while I was teaching in the evenings. Worse problems were going to present themselves in his new school holidays when he would be at home all day and I'd be at the Academy. We turned therefore to a cousin of Molly's who lived not far away. Every so often when I was up with the in-laws it was announced that Yseult was due to pay a visit. The first time I met her and after Terence had delivered his statutory greeting at the door, he said, 'There is trouble afoot, Drain'ole. You are entering a house of sorrow. Cousin Yseult is descending, I am a prisoner in my own home, we're having rabbit's food for lunch, and your son's got a face like a smacked bum.' A plan for me to take George out for the day was ruthlessly suppressed by his grandmother. I pleaded that children were often shy in front of strangers.

'Yseult is not a stranger. She's a sort of auntie.'

In point of fact, Terence was only pretending to have misgivings about these occasional descents from a woman turning out ethereally minded. 'She's a game old bird,' he said while we were waiting for her to show up. 'Ran away from home when she was still in her teens and enrolled in some mystery school in Paris. Run by a fellow who ponced about in a scarlet robe, called himself Vera or something like that.'

'Vera's a woman's name,' Mrs Davidson said.

'I'm aware of that, dear heart, that's why I said "something like that." Vivian, that was it. The school's ends were political as much as spiritual. More so, I believe. Some sort of league of nations, that's what they had in mind, to be run by initiates, though who those initiates were to be apart from themselves of course and what sort of mumbo-jumbo they laid claim to, she won't say. Vivian's pupils were all young ladies. Knobbed some of them, I shouldn't wonder, Yseult included, for all we know. One doesn't like to enquire.'

'And I hope you will not,' Mrs Davidson said.

Along with Terence, Molly anticipated these reunions with a certain degree of pleasure, although from a different angle, looking on her cousin's visits as diverting her, however temporarily, from arcane delusions. 'Poor Yseult has her head full of these odd ideas,' she said without elaborating on the peculiarity of her relative's thought processes except to say that she was of the opinion that we all came back to earth in another life, 'whether as frogs or as people I was nervous of discussing for fear of being tired out with her spooky theories. It'll do her good to get away from her awful little flat. There are mice, you know. Fancy living all alone like that, I mean to say.'

What did Molly mean to say? This was never made clear. Perhaps she meant to say only that her opinions were open to revision: that what she meant to say differed from, was even radically opposed to, what she had just put into words and that this advancement of her disapproval of a single life should not be taken as an insinuation that my own solitary existence was as reprehensible as her cousin's. Following on from that, on the other hand, she may have meant to say it was about time I surrendered my independence and took George off her hands. She had always allowed me a certain leeway in her vocal criticisms of my course of conduct because, as she once remarked, I'd never been quite the same since I'd 'gone funny.'

It occurred to me that an opportunity might arise in the course of Yseult's visit, maybe over the vegetable lunch if conversation flagged, to question her about her spiritual life that Terence had sketched out as eccentrically pursued. I still harboured a glimmer of hope that I could somehow communicate with my wife although ever since my boyhood days, when Major Scott had so violently disparaged spiritualism as disgusting nonsense, I had been in two minds about risking any further engagement. I was especially anxious to hear Yseult's theory of reincarnation and planned to ask her if rebirth might sometimes take place fairly soon after death. I could not of course express in front of the in-laws a hope that Ann might have already been reborn and that in about twenty years or so when I would be only sixty-three we might meet again. I raised the question in general terms. Yseult was delighted with my interest. Terence and George were pleased too, because her exposition, which was delivered at some length, gave them the opportunity to slip away and watch the football on television.

Meeting Yseult occasionally and listening to her esoteric ideas, delivered in a surprisingly loud voice that I had not yet interpreted as a symptom of an acute deafness, was a very different matter from having her around my own place, day in, day out, when her otherworldliness proved trying. Indeed, it is hard to write about Yseult without sounding rather a heel. All the same, Molly's proposition that spiritual concerns overrode household commitments to the point when her flat had become infested with mice, proved to be grounded in fact. She turned out a clumsy, messy, scatter-brained, woman. She did a certain amount of washing, ironing, cleaning, but she washed and ironed and cleaned with her head in mystical clouds. George and I soon relieved her of the cooking. Auntie Salt, as George named her, was the strictest of vegetarians. Her austerity did not stretch to Adam Lindsay Gordon's Norman Baron in his poem, 'Ashtaroth', whose 'rye-bread was flavoured with bitter herbs and his draught from the tasteless spring.' That would be to over-emphasise what still has to be recorded as an unappetising plainness in the Yseultian diet. She was happy to have been relieved of kitchen chores, dreamily ate whatever of our food she could assimilate and drank our tea while warming her hands around the mug and staring blankly into its depths so that, with her lank hair and abstracted gaze, she looked for all the world as if, wrapped in blankets, she had been rescued by lifeboatmen from icy waters.

She had written poetry, published by the same provincial house that had issued Ganson's verses after the publisher had read a poem of hers, entitled *A Wasp in My Jam Jar*, in a small magazine that printed poetry by women only. George, who found poetry tiresome, remarked that if she had put the top on her jam she wouldn't have had to go to the bother of writing a poem. Ganson, on the other hand, who met her a couple of times, spoke highly of the composition. 'A woman's answer to Lawrence's *The Snake*', that was his opinion. I was nervous about having brought the two together for fear that Yseult's flights of fancy on the after-life, rebirth, other sub-divisions of her hermetic creed, could include a mention of the planet Mercury and its inhabitants which were given some space in one of the six volumes (by her own admission hard to follow) laying out the doctrine to which she subscribed and so recalling to Ganson his unhappy experience in America. According to Yseult, Mercurians – the Lords of Flame – had once peopled Earth and helped the human race to establish itself. Then, as modern history began, they had taken off again for their own planet, leaving only a skeleton staff to oversee progress. Perhaps the adepts enthralling Ganson's American student had been among those who stayed behind.

There were not many days when Yseult did not refer to these spiritual beliefs, at the same time giving notice she was not at all particular which faith people followed, with the exception of any that advocated punitive measures for the unbeliever. 'In whichever temple you find yourself, honour the gods therein' was a motto she recommended. The revival of religious oppression in today's world was held by Yseult to epitomise the last lash of the Fish's tail – she spoke astrologically – before mankind moved into the age of Aquarius.

It wouldn't be unfair to say that while she was with us her regime was sometimes supplemented by a brisk administration of the Piscean flail. There were times when we were brought to heel. Neither George nor I could be certain that Yseult would not turn conversation from the light-hearted to the profound, a transference that implied we had forgotten, she hoped only temporarily, the purpose for which we had been put on earth. We must have always before our eyes the radiancy of a future when temporal concerns such as George and I were talking about – cricket included, she told him, despite his insistence that cricket was as valid a religion as any other – will have become superfluous in the state of perfected humanity predicted in Victorian times by the woman whose creed she followed.

Mary Baker Eddy may have outgunned Madame Helena Petrovna Blavatsky. Otherwise one looked in vain for a more thrusting female avatar. Her credentials had been set out between the covers of two stout volumes later expanded by four others developing articles of faith no less enigmatically presented than in the first two. The Truth behind existence: that was what she claimed to have discovered. The word was spelled with a capital throughout these texts, incorporated also within the religion's motto: 'There is no religion higher than Truth.' I once challenged Yseult concerning the accusations of cheating aimed at her famous foundress whose so-called miracles according to the scientific men and women who investigated them flouted the laws of nature. 'Quite,' Yseult said curtly, 'that is, if one goes by their narrow postulates of those laws.'

This now irretrievably forgotten creed had found its adherents at much the same time as had spiritualism, an equally *passé*, if less ostentatiously middle-class, allegiance to which however it seemed to owe a certain similarity. I put this to Yseult who could not agree. She denied that the dead returned in the form they had assumed on earth or that they spoke in the same earthly tongues. The immortal soul, she went on, resides in the pineal gland and, after death, passes out through the cranium and awaits the opportunity of a new and suitable rebirth.

This is how it comes about that we sometimes recall our past lives. Some members of our race, a very small number indeed, elect, after death, to return to the body. Their mission is to guide mankind to the Truth, very occasionally and only in extraordinary circumstances altering the course of worldly events. Of these highly developed souls, she said she could speak no more at present except to say they would certainly not manifest themselves to a spiritualist medium. Mediums were deceived by a variety of tiresome elementals with time on their hands. One afternoon over our tea I asked if those interventionists were the spirits of stream and woodland mentioned by Amos in my table-turning days. Yseult thought not. 'Far more undesirable,' she said. 'I am glad you gave up that sort of thing. It is a nasty world to muddle with and it demonstrates the occult Truth that when you knock on the gates of heaven it is the gates of hell that open first. By ineluctable law. And here comes little George.'

George had sat beside her and offered her a crisp.

'What are these, dear?'

'Crisps, auntie.'

'I don't think I know them.'

'You must have eaten crisps.'

'Must I, dear? Well, perhaps I have.' She ate one ruminatively.

'Very nice. Did you win at the football?'

'Cricket, auntie.'

'Perhaps later.'

George repeated what he had said, more loudly this time. It was of no avail.

It is generally and unkindly agreed that deaf people are a tiresome bunch. Deafness, alone of other afflictions, attracts little sympathy since it annoys the sufferer's friends more than the sufferers themselves, often making a joke of their disability, or, in Yseult's case, hardly aware there is anything amiss. The problem is two-fold: having to shout at the friend who is deaf and being shouted at back. It was my opinion that Yseult's deafness might well have been self-induced, oblivion to the outside world found to assist concentration upon the inner life. She caught us out once. George asked me where she was.

'Gone up to heaven in a fiery chariot.'

From the next room, Yseult called back: 'Not just yet, dear.'

Out of doors, she found hearing even more difficult than at home.

That did not stop her talking loudly enough to startle people nearby. Mostly she would pick up on a thread of mystical submissions forwarded earlier in the day, her high-pitched words informing those around her of the certitude of a higher existence or of her conception of the Veil of Nothingness, phrases that might well have been received with some trepidation as introductory to this madwoman's calling for silence and presenting to all who cared to listen, come to that to those who did not care, an exegesis on the Masters and the Path.

These challenges are no more than excuses for one's own confusion at finding oneself in public with a slightly odd, deaf, abstracted, woman who, for all that, possessed a good deal more intelligence than those one was worried she was startling. For instance, I would have welcomed more information (if not necessary publicly expounded) on our final destiny about which Yseult was strangely reticent. So far as could be gathered, the human race ought by rights to be striving for perfection and was indeed slowly making its way towards this idealistic state. When it had been achieved, we would have all become hermaphroditic. Procreation of the human race would become possible without a partner, so absolving us from the degradation of sexual intercourse. It was an aspiration worth considering. While not agreeing with Yseult's prudery, I had often thought that sex and love had nothing much to do with each other. In furtherance of this idealistic struggle, Yseult said, we were helped on our way by an elect body of men – never women, it seemed – well advanced along the Path who had chosen to be reborn time and again to oversee, guide, instruct, in very rare cases manifest themselves to human beings. These were the Masters. Two such perfected beings hailed from India, a continent in one of George's books of legerdemain known as the Mystic East, peopled to his way of thinking with men – again, never women – who performed the Indian Rope Trick, lay on beds of nails, vomited scorpions. This conflicting viewpoint, not of course expressed in words by either George or myself, was the eventual cause of Yseult's departure.

The paramountcy to Yseult of her Masters was made apparent when she appeared to me once at dead of night. She had asked if she might stay over for a few days. The reason given for this temporary change of lodging was that her flat was in urgent need of re-wiring. It had become a safety risk, or so Terence had warned. He moved in to undertake the electrical work. That was only half the story. There was another, hidden, more urgent, agenda laid down by Molly, an extermination, or at the very least a serious cull, of the mouse population in Yseult's flat which had become unmanageable owing to her tolerance of the invaders, now extended to hospitality by her provision for them of saucers of food and milk. As well as the rewiring, Terence was ordered to implement the rodent operation. He had protested that it was a job for professionals but Molly forbade this logical objection because she was alarmed that a qualified pest controller would be likely to roll up in a van advertising his calling and so alerting Yseult's neighbours to her unhygienic lifestyle.

She made her spectral appearance at two in the morning, presenting as close to a stereotyped apparition as was possible: ectoplasmic gown, trailing hair, whispered words. Yseult had stood at the foot of my bed, breathing a prayer to her Masters that I might throw off the shackles of my profanity and tread in future the pathway to the Truth. At least that was what seemed to prompt the visitation. Later on, I changed my mind about the motive behind Yseult's prayers to the extent that I was relieved when she turned against us and walked out of our lives.

One day, she awoke from one of her teacup trances, screwed up her eyes as she often did and announced she was going to London. This was unusual. She did not often venture further than walking distances, sometimes taking George with her on nature rambles. She had been brought up by her military grandfather and a scatterbrained mother who between them had inculcated in her a sense of wonderment for every branch of creation, especially the love for God's lowlier creatures that had stirred her to feed her mice and to write *A Wasp in my Jam Jar*. Her passion for pond life left George cold, conceding only a fascination for some leeches discovered on a country walk when he said Yseult had 'gone on' about fritillaries. Her London plan was to call in at her lawyers and then visit some art galleries.

George volunteered to go with her. He reported on an eventful day. He was grateful that Yseult didn't hold his hand as I insisted upon doing in busy places because I was for ever nervous of losing him in a crowd. Yseult had walked the city pavements in the manner she walked about the house, as if she trod the deck of a seagoing vessel, every so often falling sideways when her boat pitched in heavy waters. She had bumped into several people along the way.

'People she knew?'

'No. By mistake. She never says sorry.'

Something odd had happened, George said. In an art gallery she had cannoned into a man who had instigated a very different reaction from Yseult's usual obliviousness to having been the cause of a collision. She had fallen to her knees.

'Fell over?'

'No, kneeled down like in church.'

'Perhaps she was just going to do up your shoelaces.'

'No, my shoelaces were done up as a matter of fact. And I wasn't doing anything I shouldn't.'

'You hadn't done any spinning around.'

'Well, I did spin a little, I suppose. Because I was a bit bored. Nothing for her to get alarmed about. She was going on about Crack something.'

'Cranach, the painter?'

'No.'

'Cracked, like you?'

'That's not funny.'

'It's funny a bit.'

'It's not funny lots.'

'Craquelure?'

'Might have been. Then she knelt down in front of this man as if she'd tripped over but hadn't. She didn't say sorry to bother you or anything like that, just held the man's hand and stared up at him and and did her funny squeezing up bit with her eyes. She said "Master."'

'What did the man do?'

'Just smiled and pulled her up and buzzed off super fast. He had funny grey hair, no, white, tied up at the back. Bit gay, basically. Auntie Salt came all over funny after that. We had to go straight home, she said. She was all out of breath and panting and looking weird. I thought she might die on the train and I'd have to pull the communication cord. Then when we got back here she lay down on the stairs with her head pointing downwards. She said it was good for feeling faint and that she'd read it in a book. She showed it me when she got better. It's called *Enquire Within Upon Everything*. There's something in it you need to make a note of. As a father.' George found his tablet and read from the screen: '"Paragraph 920. Over-Work. Late hours and anxious pursuits exhaust the nervous system, and produce disease and premature death. Therefore, the hours of labour and study should be short."' George laid

74

stress on the last sentence.

Yseult's eventual departure came about because of a conjuring performance given by George whose interest in the art had turned to a passion, the result of a chance meeting in the café downstairs on one of his grandparents' visits. The incident needs recording for its bearing on future events. These days, when the in-laws came down, they put up at a local hotel, Terence now finding the return drive home too tiring to manage in a day.

'Just coming up to the ten to,' Terence said, looking at his watch.

'Time for a cocktail?' Molly asked.

'If you say so, but I wasn't aware you knew any.'

'Don't be silly, Terence.'

'Yes, let's have a cocktail, my love. It will put some wool in our needles.'

On the ground floor of my building was a tea-shop, Astracote favoured by Molly who praised the ginger cakes, freshly baked on the premises. Recently, in an intended up-grade, management had decided to stay open in the evening and had made some moves to turn the tea-shop into a wine-bar. After about five o'clock, curtains were pulled across the windows, lights were lowered, the sugar-pots replaced with small lighted tapers. The walls had been hung with framed photographs of celebrities from an era certainly well before my own, even before the in-laws', nevertheless of some appeal to Molly who enjoyed trying to identify as many as she could from whichever seat she was occupying at the time. She had compiled quite a list, Bernard Shaw, Zsa-Zsa Gabor, Clark Gable, a New York mayor of prohibition days. On this particular evening, she and Terence began quarreling about who was represented among the pictures.

'Whatever possessed them to put up Myra Hindley?'

Molly asked for the photograph to be pointed out. 'What a juggins you are, Terence. That's Carole Lombard.'

'Well, she looks like Myra Hindley.' He sipped at his martini. 'Is this Billie Holiday we've got singing? Am I the only person who dislikes that tiresome little voice? I suppose she's out of copyright. That would explain why you hear her everywhere you go. The only thing about her records that makes them bearable is Lester Young's saxophone. I'm going to ask for her to be turned off.'

I hoped this mutual tetchiness would stop when the drinks took hold. I looked about me. At a nearby table two men were playing cards. One was elderly and wore a Tyrolean hat, the other was young, bare-headed, fair-haired, open-faced, undeniably good-looking. I was sitting directly behind the elder player which made it impossible for me to see what game was in progress. Poker seemed the most likely although they did not appear to be playing for money. From the old fellow's point of view, that was a good thing because his friend, for all his inoffensiveness, was cheating.

All that could be heard from our table was the slap of the cards as the players bent to their game. The jaunty feather in the older man's hat, the light cast over the scene deriving from variant angles and illuminating the cheek of the younger player and the seamed neck of the older, recalled Caravaggio's 'The Cardsharps', although the artist's third, non-playing, figure, accomplice of the plume-wearing contestant, was absent from the scene. Card-sharping was what was now in progress. Breaking into the quiet concentration of the players there could be detected an unnatural rhythm as the younger man dealt his opponent's hands. Every so often the slap of the cards was appreciably louder. This was because he was dealing unfairly. The cards he dealt came from the bottom of the pack.

The bottom deal is not an easy sleight to perform undetectably, especially with a full pack. The buckling of the bottom card by the fingers of the left hand which ideally should never leave the cards' outside edges, the masking of the action by its thumb's pushing across of the top card the dealer is feigning to pass over the table and its withdrawal a split second later as the right hand moves to take the loosened substitute are difficult movements to synchronize. The blond fellow had slightly disguised an imperfect timing by turning his left wrist as he made the false move. The accentuated snap or sometimes an extended slithering sound as the card was passed out were indications that trickery was afoot.

The in-laws continued to bicker. A top-hatted figure on the wall had been picked out for identification.

'That's Romilly Lunge,' Molly said. Terence asked how she knew.

'I recognize him.'

'How can you recognize him? He was well before your time. You couldn't possibly have seen Romilly Lunge either on the stage or in pictures. He probably died before you were born. Retired from films, anyway.'

76

'I'm not saying I saw him. Not contemporaneously, so to speak. But it doesn't mean I couldn't have seen him in an old feature they showed on the television or gone to a cinema where they put on vintage films. My grandmother used to say what an attractive man he was. One can see it in this photo, of course.'

'What would that blepharitic old laundry-list know about masculine good looks?'

'Don't speak of my grandmother in that way, please, Terence. A woman you hardly knew.'

'Luckily for me. Well, if you tell me that's Romilly Lunge, then who am I to contradict you, dearest heart. We mustn't quarrel in front of our son-in-law. Mind you, it was always said of Romilly Lunge that he was an out-and-out...'

'That's quite enough, Terence.'

'Well, I'm only saying.'

'Then don't say. I am sure that whatever you were going to tell us would have been both unpleasant and uncalled-for. Oh, now I remember the title of that film of his. I saw him in *The Gods of...*'

Gods of what? Of which church? Of what faith? What country? Which planet? Perhaps of Mercury, this old-time science-fiction film recalled by Molly ratifying in black-and-white photography her cousin Yseult's belief of Mercurian descent onto earth? That was never revealed. At that moment the café lights went out. It seemed as if the disturbing currents flying between my in-laws had blown the electrical circuit. More prosaically, this was a common occurrence that affected as well the lighting in my flat upstairs run from a communal fusebox in the café's basement. The fault, although fixable temporarily once an electrician was called in, had never been permanently remedied.

Terence got up. 'Hold on a tick. There's a simple answer to this,' he said. He hurried out.

Someone, in Terence's waggish vein, called out, 'Where was Moses when the lights went out.' One of the card-players, the dupe of the fair-headed manipulator, gave the correct answering call, 'In the dark.' There was laughter. The proprietress came round with extra candles. Some people were illuminating their tables with the lights from their telephones. 'What a good idea,' Molly said. 'I've got my 'phone in my bag somewhere. Aren't they fiddly things? I'm hopeless with them. Terence does all my ringing up for me.'

'I'm so worried about him,' she went on. She spoke in low tones as did all the bar customers who interpreted that the darkness, that was indeed intensifying sounds including the pronounced slap of the card-cheat's bottom deal, might encourage eavesdroppers. 'He gets confused. That's why he won't drive much any more. He says he forgets where he's meant to be going. And, oh dear, this constant telling us all what time it is, I mean to say. I do hope he won't have to be put away. I don't know what I'd do without him.' Molly took my hand.

I assured her that Terence was perfectly well. It had not occurred to me that she relied on him nor, indeed, it was now revealed, that she was very fond of him. When I thought about it, it was Molly I preferred to Terence whose banter I found exasperating in the extreme.

Then, the door was thrown violently open. Someone, an electrician, or perhaps a police officer, so peremptorily did he propel the beam of a powerful flashlight around the darkened room, was making his way slowly and purposefully among the gathering. His torch picked us out table by table, resting for some time upon the two gamesters who shielded their eyes from its piercing rays, as if in an illicit gambling-den they were hoping to conceal their identity from a brutal law-enforcer. It was not long before it was Molly's turn and mine to be isolated in the bullseye lantern, blinding us with its glare. For the first time a voice spoke. 'Hello, dad.'

George stood there. He was in his pyjamas. His feet were bare.

'What on earth are you doing? You are meant to be in bed.'

'I was, but then grand-dad said I was to get up and come down and mend the lights. I mended them before, remember?' The proprietress came over. A tableau now composed itself in the candlelit bar, an effigial tableau of some noteworthy moment in history displayed in a wax museum about to close for the night, a scene that in its arresting qualities matched any of the stills from the old films that adorned the café's walls. Terence, who had entered behind his grandson, stood beside him with an arm thrown protectively across his shoulders. Man and boy faced a wardress, her hands on her hips, a bunch of keys dangling from her waist, as if this fiercest of turnkeys was determined against Terence's will to seize hold of his small companion and lock him in her dungeon. Defiance from the three parties prevented all motion. Then George hitched up his pyjamas, collapsing a scene that had sustained considerable dramatic strength.

78

'I'm not at all sure...,' the café owner protested.

'He is rather a dab hand at this sort of thing,' Terence said.

'One wouldn't want him to electrocute himself.'

'One would not. But he won't.'

'Well, if you're sure.'

With the return of the lights came a burst of applause as George appeared from wherever the fusebox was secreted and padded on his bare feet to our table. I told him about the card sharp and alerted him to the giveaway 'slither' of the cards. George thought he might be a conjuror rather than a shyster and was about to go over and confront him when an ice-cream sundae of mammoth proportions made its appearance in a fluted glass. 'With the compliments of the management,' the waitress said. Before this reward could be tackled, Molly insisted George should go upstairs and 'put some proper clothes on. You can't sit about in a smart wine-bar in your jimbos. Whatever will people think, I mean to say.'

As George passed the gamblers' table, the younger of the two men called out 'Good night, sleep tight.' George halted, pulled out a spare chair, and sat down, motioning the man to pass over his pack of cards. He was two tricks into what could have devolved into a lengthy routine before I got up and sent him on his way upstairs.

'I've been rumbled then?' the man said.

I apologized for George's interruption. The man introduced himself as Kit Buller. We began to talk. He was not a card sharp. He was a conjuror, as George had supposed, and he had been teaching a mutual enthusiast the bottom deal. He introduced his elderly pupil who stood up, clicked his heels and removed his hat. I recognized Klaus Muller, the Academy's German professor. He managed a smile. He seemed put out by my appearance as if he had been revealed to this work colleague of his whom he did not know at all well as owning to a hobby conceivable as being on the childish side for a mature academician to indulge. He gave me no more than a curt good evening, adding that he had not seen me before in this establishment.

For some reason Goethe's phrase about a wine-shop I had translated for Drake came to mind, *Ja, in der Schenke hab ich auch geseßen*, 'Yes, in the tavern I too have been seated' in Edward Dowden's translation. I repeated Goethe's German to Herr Muller, thinking that a reply in his own language might put him more at his ease. I had intended to explain how I came to know these lines, saying I was a friend of his pupil who had asked me for a possible translation of *Schenke*.

Muller cut me short. He said, 'I wasn't aware it was that sort of a bar'. He pawed the air with a limp hand. His gesture permitted of only one interpretation.

'Are you saying that Goethe enjoyed sitting around in gay bars?'

'Well, the Persian poet he's translating is saying so.' Muller sat down again and began an overhand shuffle, neatly injogging a central card to ensure his top stock remained in a specified order. He cut the pack and turned over the first card. It was the ace of spades. 'Bingo. Yes, in his notes to the poem, Goethe writes that the bar's cup-bearers as he calls them, by which he means the juvenile personnel of the establishment, only a bit older than that boy of yours, were available for dalliance. He hastily adds that, in accordance with current morals, those, that is to say, that perpended in his country at the time he was writing, the subject needs to be treated with decency. He further adds a note that wine-bibbing moderately indulged and a mutual inclination between men and youths that he refers to as pedagogy are not to be discouraged. Some critics suggest that Goethe was of like persuasion.'

Mr Buller remarked on how good he thought George's two tricks were. 'Of course, we conjurors mustn't say tricks. We must call them "effects".'

'I remember that. I'm not much of a magician but I seem to have turned my son into some sort of fanatic.'

'I was never quite good enough to make it professionally. I became a soldier instead. If ever your son wants a spot of tuition I'd be very pleased to volunteer. He's very talented, you know. What is his name?'

As things turned out, Kit became an established part of George's routine. He'd bicycle over to Kit's place for magical instruction once or twice a week: oftener as the day approached when he was billed to perform at the Aldhouses' daughter's birthday party. A final dress rehearsal for this event was arranged. Auntie Salt and I were to be among the audience. Kit would be present as a backstage assistant.

It was about this time that I discovered Yseult did not live entirely on the exalted sphere that absolved her from the human, to her way of thinking, unworthy, susceptibilities to which most of us are prey. There lodged within her one primitive need that she had not been able to conquer, one that suggested her infiltration into our household,

80

George's and mine, owed much to this atavistic urge no longer under her control. On a morning drawing near to George's magical perfor- mance, she and I were banished to the downstairs café because George needed the sitting-room for a semi-final dress rehearsal of his act. Yseult looked up from the depths of her teacup. She stared at me for a long time before she spoke. 'Have you ever thought that George might like a little companion?'

'He has this great friend, Cyrus.'

'I mean of his own flesh and blood.'

'That could hardly be.'

'I still have my courses.'

It took a while longer than it took Yseult to blow on her tea, screw up her eyes and then open them wide again and project over the table a sudden arching of the eyebrows for the appalling implication of her words to suppurate into consciousness. The contemplation of Yseult's menstrual cycles compounded horrifically with a revulsion at being the agent for their cessation. The hour for her departure had sounded. She must never again set foot in my house. The problem was how she was to be removed. As luck would have it, George's final rehearsal brought it about.

A reasonably priced programme of events announced an afternoon of 'Definitely Different Deceptions.' These were to be presented by 'Prince Kasan, Master Magician of the Orient.' I, Yseult, and a couple of George's school friends sat in darkness. Flutes, playing offstage and increasing in volume and sinuosity as the lights came up, endorsed George's talents with the café's electricity supply. A cymbal clashed. Smoke billowed through the open hallway door. George appeared. He had dressed up. Indisputably Indian characteristics, high caste and low, maharajah and yogi, had been blended into one personality. Spacious pantaloons, possibly Yseult's pyjama bottoms – substituted in cooler weather for the nightgown in which I had seen her ethereally clad when praying to the Masters at my bedroom door – proposed an altogether mean- er stamp than the wide purple cummerbund from which they were suspended and the bejewelled turban surmounting George's head. To underline exotic origins George's face, torso, arms, and feet had been awarded a rich chestnut coating.

He had forbidden applause, often merited throughout a pretty good show, good enough to have deserved a larger audience than our small assembly. The act sometimes diverged from the implied oriental atmosphere, for instance in the Appearing Walking Stick and a comedy item, Magic Washing, in which silk handkerchiefs, securely tied to a clothes line by Yseult, deferentially salaamed onto the stage by the Prince, amazingly broke free from their moorings in the high wind that she was encouraged to imitate by shaking the ropes while thunder rolled from George's sound system and fluttered to the ground. His closing effect returned to the fakir persona proposed upon entry. Six large darning needles were ingested one by one, helped down George's throat by draughts of water magically produced from a jug demonstrably proved empty only a moment before. A line of thread pulled from a reel of white cotton followed the needles down the wonderworker's gullet. There was some writhing about while this fearsome repast was digested. Sinuous music again infringed. Kit dimmed the lights leaving only a viridian beam to play on George's face as he delicately regurgitated the end of the cotton strand to produce the needles one by one, each neatly threaded onto the cotton and sparkling in the spotlight's glow.

Clapping was now permitted; a curtain call bashfully taken. Yseult did not join in the applause. She sat with pursed lips, then rose and gave a totter as she often did when getting to her feet: lurched from the room.

Kit came in. I congratulated him on his magical tuition.

'What's up with George's auntie?'

'She probably just didn't get it,' George said. 'She doesn't get a lot of things. She made a bit of a mess with the knots in Magic Washing.'

'That's women for you,' Kit remarked.

'You put George up to it.' Yseult faced me across the kitchen table.

'To what?'

'To making a mockery of my beliefs. You know quite well our Masters hail from India.'

'I thought you said they came from central Europe.'

'The European is an exception. He is on a different ray. If I thought your steps were on the Path I would tell you how close he is to all of us at this moment. But you have proved yourself unworthy and are leading little George into the same unworthy ways. You encouraged him to portray our Masters as frauds, tricksters. Trickery: that is what we have been accused of since our foundation. Our very founder was foully and wrongly accused of trickery. Righteousness on the Path can sometimes lead to miracles as I have tried to explain to you and little George, but you have set him against me. I am disappointed.'

Those were her last words. In the evening, George and I watched her walk unsteadily down the road weighed down with two laundry bags into which she had packed the six volumes of her book of faith. She set off with firm tread, her constitutionally weaving walk anchored by the two heavy bags from one of which a stocking detached itself and dropped on the pavement. She did not notice. George was about to run after her and pick it up: then stopped and instead turned to me and threw his arms round my waist.

'Dad, can I say something important?'

'Of course.'

'Let's not ever have anyone else coming between us.'

'No, let's not.'

CHAPTER V

There was something to be said in favour of Ganson's SWOT programme, at least to judge from the audience awaiting me for my first lecture on the poetry of Adam Lindsay Gordon. I had almost a full house. I was nearly late arriving for the class because of an unsettling incident in the street not far from the Academy where a man was being questioned by two policemen. The suspect was dishevelled, distraught, engaging noisily with the officers. It was Terence.

I went over. Terence gave no sign of recognition.

'Do you know this man, sir?'

'He is my father-in-law.'

The officer was not convinced. 'And what is your father-in-law's name?'

'Davidson.'

'This man says his name is Ezneret.'

'That is Terence, pronounced backwards. He is Terence Davidson. I am Leonard Saunders, known to Mr Davidson as Drain'ole which, by the same token, is Leonard backwards.'

The policeman looked me up and down as if I, as well as Mr Ezneret, might be classified as being unfit to be at large in a public thoroughfare.

'Drain'ole.' Terence shook himself free from a restraining grasp and clapped me on the shoulder. 'Am I glad to see you. I am in a bit of a fix.'

Explanations offered by Terence and the two policemen constructed an odd tale. Terence, who could provide no motive for being in the town, certainly not for the purpose of visiting me and George, had got it into his head that his wristwatch was out of order. Not that it had stopped. The hands, he declared, were in the wrong place. They had been moved by unseen forces. He had asked one of the two officers for the correct time and, when it was confirmed to be the same as that showing on his watch, had levelled an accusation that the informant and his colleague, who had by this time shown up to see what the fuss was about, were party to some sort of conspiracy – Terence thought of Russian, perhaps Chinese, origin – aimed at disrupting the United Kingdom in readiness for further provocative cyber attacks upon our peaceable nation.

After a short debate, it was agreed by the three of us who had, as it were, come to Terence's rescue, that he had been the subject of some lapse of reason from which he appeared to have recovered and that if I would now take responsibility for him everybody could be on his way. Terence too was coming round to the idea that he had suffered no more than a temporary blackout and accompanied me quietly to my room in college, stopping en route to buy a takeaway cup of tea and a currant bun.

'I'd love to come and hear your lecture, Drain'ole.'

'You'd be bored to tears. Sit here. Switch on the radio. The cricket starts in five minutes.'

'Can one smoke?'

'Of course. I'll be back in an hour.'

For my first lecture on Adam Lindsay Gordon I had chosen one of his longer poems, *The Romance of Britomarte*. Britomarte was a horse, a fearless charger named after the Cretan nymph in Spenser's *Faerie Queene*. The poem begins:

> I'll tell you a story, but pass the 'jack'
> And let us make merry tonight, my men.

Time was spent discussing whether the word 'jack' in the first line referred to a leather bottle, a meaning a student had turned up in the dictionary or whether it was short for applejack. It was thought the bottle was the more likely of the two given that applejack, a drink of American origin, as another class member pointed out, had not been imported into the England of the Protectorate, the period in which the narrative was set. It was a rousing story of cavaliers versus roundheads, the narrator, Ralph Leigh, a stalwart royalist. Many years ago when his beard was black, so he tells his mates sitting around a table and quaffing from the 'jack', he had been a servant, employed at St Hubert's Chase, a noble seat, in those civil war days besieged by Roundhead forces. At the request of the house's orphaned owner, Gwendoline (her father, Sir Hugh, had been slain at Edgehill) with whom the aging trooper had played in the Chase's grounds when they were both children as if they were social equals despite Ralph's lowly birth, he saddles his mare, Britomarte, and rides out in search of a rescuing force. I explained that Britomart was a nymph from the isle of Crete much given to hunting, passing over Gordon's eccentric spelling that had been noted by Ganson in one of his disparagements of Gordon's poetry. Ralph locates a Royalist garrison under the command of a nobleman, 'stately and stern' Sir

Guy, alerts him to the peril looming over the Chase, and begs him to order his troops to relieve it. Avoiding all perils, Britomarte gallops back in company with Sir Guy's men-at-arms. The Chase is saved but, tragically, after her exhausting run, 'brave Britomarte lay dead in her stall' and Ralph Leigh, badly wounded, takes to his sickbed. He was far from well:

> Three weeks I slept at St Hubert's Chase.
> When I woke from the fever of wounds and wine
> I could scarcely believe that the ghastly face
> The glass reflected was really mine.

He discovers that Sir Guy and Gwendoline have been married while he was lying ill. Gwendoline asks what reward he would like for relieving the Chase. He begs a lock of her hair.

> I took it maybe more than enough
> And I shore it rudely close to the roots.
> For the wounds and the wine had made me rough
> And men at the bottom are merely brutes.

I asked the students if they could think of any other narrative poem beginning in much the same way, drawing in the listener with the promise of a good yarn. Someone mentioned *The Ancient Mariner*, another the ghost's exhortation in *Hamlet*, 'I could a tale unfold ...' My brightest spark was able to quote Jonson's epigram, 'Weep with me, all you that read this little story.' Then a young man in jeans and a Voivod T-shirt got to his feet. I knew him as Ray, often to be seen out in the street before lectures began, dragging on a roll-up cigarette. He was alleged to be a reformed cider drinker, banned in perpetuity, Fred had told me, from the Jolly Herring. 'Don't address me as Raymond,' he once appealed to me. 'It's what my mum calls me when I've done something wrong.' Ray announced that he knew by heart a poem that began with the exact words of *The Legend of Britomarte*.

' "I'll tell you a story," ' he said.

'Go on.'

'I'm not sure I ought to, Mr Saunders. The composition is of a racy nature.'

'We're all fairly open-minded.'

'Well, if you're sure.' Raymond stood up and climbed onto his chair.

86

He quoted the opening lines:

> I'll tell you a story that's certain to please
> Of a grand farting contest at Burton-on-Tees.

Some sort of protest seemed in order but I was shouted down by the class's insistence on Raymond's declamation of his poem from start to finish. It was of considerable length, during which I wondered if the public house ban came about because of just such a recital. Had Raymond, flushed with his cider, clambered unsteadily onto a chair or a table, called for silence, and begun a slurred rendering of *The Grand Farting Contest* before Fred put him out on his ear? The recitation drew loud applause and some noises imitative of the burden of Raymond's lay. I spoke briefly about Chaucer's bawdy: Herrick's. Another student, a woman this time, raised her hand. Just then, the Dean put his head round the door.

'Everything all right?'

'Yes.'

'Sounded like a riot from outside.' Ganson shut the door behind him. He was probably thinking of 'sitting in.'

'I've nearly finished, Dean. I'll just hear what this student has to say.'

'My name's Gwendoline, like her in the Gordon poem. And the funny thing is, I'm going to get married in three weeks' time and the man I'm like marrying's called Sir Guy. So it'll be like "the wedding of Guy and of Gwendoline."'

The class cheered. Someone asked for Guy's surname. On hearing the answer, Ganson's bald head shone. He stepped forward, raised his hands to bring a respectful silence to the room and he said: 'Let us show our appreciation to Mr Saunders for what I am sure, from your shining faces, was a fascinating lecture. next week he'll be talking to us about the verse novels of Gilbert Frankau.'

After the applause and the dismissal of the assembly, Ganson turned to me and said: 'Come to my office.'

I said: 'I've got to look after my father-in-law. He's in my room. He's feeling unwell.'

Ganson was not to be deterred. 'Be quick about it, then. What I want to say is of signal importance.'

'I won't be long.'

Terence had gone. He had left a note: 'Dear D: Thanks for your rescue.

I can't think what came over me. O.K. now. P.S. – Not a word to Molly about this.'

Ganson was at his desk. He was still very excited. Capiscum scents wafted from him in pungent flurries. 'That student's wedding. The Academy must lay on the wedding breakfast.'

'Isn't that the bride's family's responsibility?'

'They'll be glad not to have to shoulder the cost. Her husband-to-be, Sir Guy Wendon, is a local brewer, you know, and a rich man as most brewers are, and I don't imagine for a moment young Whoeversheis's tribe has got any money. What we are looking at here is a heaven-sent opportunity to ingratiate ourselves with the aristocracy and then see if we can't woo Sir Guy into lending us, giving us, well if not giving or lending then setting us up with some sort of scholarly foundation, prize, medal, award, that sort of thing, in his name. It would do the Academy a world of good, locally. Perhaps nationally.'

'A shot in the arm, then?'

Ganson took this badly. 'There's no need to make fun of these rare and happy opportunities, just because it means we all have to put our shoulders to the wheel. I'll get Stairs on to the costing. Everyone may have to forego a few days' salary but if we bring this thing off it'll be well worth the loss of a pound or two. Do you think the people on your ground floor would do the catering?'

He pressed a button on his intercom. Bailey's voice answered. In the background a sporting commentary was playing on his television. Ganson explained his new scheme. The horse race and Ganson's imaginative conspectus of the grand wedding feast with its consequent, and now to his way of thinking, inevitable affiliation of Sir Guy to the Academy came to an end at much the same time. There was a moment's silence. Then, Bailey spoke only to acknowledge that he had grasped the outline of what had been put before him.

'Godamnit, Stairs, what's wrong with you? You sound as unenthusiastic as Leonard who I've got sitting here at the moment.'

Bailey made a vague noise in his throat, its import hard to interpret. He may not have taken in everything the Dean had said, either because he was distracted by the race on which it was probable he had laid out some money or because there may have risen in his mind the moment Ganson began to unfold his blueprint that the operation would be likely to attract what he referred to as the Buggerance Factor.

Among the accoutrements of Bailey's mental office were three imaginary filing trays marked similarly to those that are depicted in humorous drawings of clerical staff at work, 'In', 'Out', and 'Pending'. To these had been added a fourth, labelled the Buggerance Factor. Possibly such a tray actually existed concealed in a dark corner of Bailey's abode, piled high with papers yellowing with age. It was likelier, however, that any communication coming under Bailey's eye, letter, memorandum, fax, text, email, that he suspected to be susceptible to the coefficient of the Buggerance Factor had been permanently deleted, shredded, consigned to the wastepaper basket.

Colin Bailey's Factor B was constituted from a standard objection of his to any supplementary enterprise that might impose upon a routine already necessitating an artful manipulation of the available hours in a day between the Academy, the Jolly Herring, and the racing calendar, the latter of which was followed on television or at the course itself, if the distance were near enough not to institute the malefic mathematics of the Buggerance Factor, and affect a second excursion to the public house and a decent night's rest.

Later on, in the Herring, Colin called Fred over.

'Frederick, a word in your shell-like. Do you stock Wendon's Ale?'

Fred shook his head.

'Ever tried it?' Colin asked.

'That I have, Mr Bailey.'

'What's it like?'

'Weasel piss,' Fred said.

CHAPTER VI

A few days afterwards, an odd incident occurred. Drake, the chauffeur and German student of Herr Muller, beckoned me over to his table. Now he had established that we were both descended from circus folk, he had become much friendlier, more inclined for a gossip, at the same time regretting that his duties forbade his prolonging this agreeable way of kicking off the morning. He remarked on progress with his German studies. He was still battling with Goethe's *West-östlicher Divan*, he said. He was amused to hear of my discovery that Dr Muller was learning card tricks. For once, he seemed not to have to hurry off to work.

'Did your nipper tell you he flagged me down on his bike yesterday? Nice lad. Well spoken, like you, of course. He asked if he could have a ride in His Nibs's car.'

George had not told me about this encounter, probably reckoning, with some justification, he'd have been ticked off for making a nuisance of himself.

'He's said nothing about it. I'm sorry he bothered you.'

'No bother, squire. Mr Welldone's all for it. Says, what about Thursday?'

'That's very kind.'

'You'd be welcome to come along as well, of course.'

'Thank you.'

It hadn't occurred to me that Drake's employer, now identified as Mr Welldone, would be accompanying us until George and I showed up at the meeting-place Drake had suggested. He occupied the back seat. It was not easy to assign an age to this man. He was small in stature with a pale dry skin suggesting that a discreet boudoir powdering had been applied before appearing in public. His pallor matched a head of white hair tied behind with a black ribbon. A high-buttoned tunic was worn in conjunction with a pair of blue jeans, a discordance of dress that recalled George's high and low caste wardrobe in his role of the Master Magician of the Orient.

George asked if he could sit next to Drake. I got into the back. Mr Welldone made no effort to move up, maintaining an upright position in the very middle of the upholstered seat as if the slightest misalignment to either side of a weight to be estimated at no more than ten stone might cause his big car to tip over. He said nothing for some time.

Then he spoke in the deepest bass voice I had ever heard, as if he had in his mouth some gadget similar to a Punch's swazzle, although of a very different pitch, an almost fraudulent gruffness that might be assumed by a youth no more than four or five years George's senior anxious to present himself to a grown-up as a contemporary, and, what's more, as a virile, companion. The German word for ventriloquist, *Bauchredner*, came to mind as Mr Welldone's words of welcome to us both – using our Christian names and agreeing that George could sit in front with the chauffeur – seemed to be generated not in the voice-box but lower in the body. Not, however in the belly, where the Germans implied the trickster's words originated but from the heart, 'from the bottom of the heart', as people say when protesting sincerity. Mr Welldone's voice had that particular warmth of expression. We rode along in this congenial mood with his asking questions about my job and progress with writing the village history about which I had to suppose Drake had filled him in although I couldn't remember mentioning my literary ambitions in our breakfast talks. Then George asked Drake how fast the car could go.

Over his shoulder Drake spoke to Mr Welldone: 'Is there time to open her up, sir?'

'Are we at home?'

I took this question, volleyed fairly sharply when one considered Mr Welldone's affability so far on the journey, to be an animadversion on Drake's line of thought, a suggestion that his mind was wandering, that he had temporarily lost control of his senses, that nobody who was in his right mind could conceive even for one moment that the owner of this valuable car was going to allow it, now or on any future occasion, to be 'opened up.'

'No, sir.'

'Then let us.'

We drove along some way further and stopped at one of the gated entrances to the grounds of the castle for which our county was famous. Drake sounded his horn. A man uniformed in blue serge appeared from a side door let into the granite wall surrounding this area, gave one look at the car, and promptly threw open the iron-studded doors that had been barring our way.

A vista of considerable beauty was revealed behind the gates, as if proscenium curtains in a grand opera-house had parted to present the audience with a painted landscape of precise formality. An unveering avenue, two or three miles in length, lay ahead. The perfect upkeep of this gravelled road which ran through ranks of equally precise chestnut trees pruned, they looked, by topiarists hoisted up on cranes, overhung the sleek raked route towards the horizon. Against the far blue backdrop of a sky presented devoid of clouds, the better to enhance its silhouette, an equestrian statue reflected bronze rays from the morning sun.

Drake revved the engine. The tyres screamed on the hard surface. We shot off at much the same top speed we achieved when only a couple of minutes later we violently braked inches from the plinth on which the chevalier with drawn sword arrogantly stared down on us as if we had dared to try and unseat from his saddle this personage of noble, most probably royal, lineage. Drake turned the car with a neat application of his reverse gear. The car descended back to the gates at the same high speed. Drake reversed once more. Up we went again.

During these furious progresses, Mr Welldone had maintained a studied calm, both hands by his side with each thumb and forefinger forming a circle, palms upright, in resemblance of a yogic *mudra*, a posture he may have learned in a school of Eastern disciplines to be assumed on occasions when nerves need to be kept under control. Drake reversed us and drove us furiously back to our starting point by the gatekeeper's lodge.

'That's enough, I think, Drake.' George pleaded for one more journey. 'Very well but your father and I who are nervously disposed will alight and sit on this bench.'

Drake got out and opened the passenger door. Upright, Mr Welldone turned out to be taller by far than I had conceived, the descent from his car into a standing position by its side suddenly, almost unaccountably, elasticising to a fair degree the nearly miniature figure he had represented sitting down. Drake and George swooped away on their third journey to the statue on the hill.

'I was educated at the same school as Adam Lindsay Gordon.' Mr Welldone patted the bench as a sign I should sit beside him. He continued to treat me with perfect politeness, at the same time as implying a natural seniority of both rank and age. 'Almost as briefly as he, although I was not, as he was, expelled for riding racehorses. Then, as you know, he went on to a military academy where he met with a relation of mine,

Thomas Bland Strange.'

'Gunner Jingo?'

'Yes. That's the man. Only a distant cousin. Someone to be proud of though.'

The car dashed past us, slewed round, threw up gravel, and began a fourth run towards the bronze horseman. George must have persuaded Drake to perform yet another circuit. A nagging anxiety that this lap, which I must surely insist on being the last, might result in the machine's crashing into the statue and sending horse and rider tumbling in smithereens to the ground, prevented my asking Mr Welldone how on earth he had become aware of my interest in Gordon. I assumed at the time, still do assume, he must have known someone on the Academy staff. Mr Welldone had spoken as if he and Gordon had been contemporaries at the school ridding itself of Gordon for his daredevil steeplechases rather than there being something like a hundred years between their attendances. This exemplified a certain otherworldliness about the man's conversation to which, as time went on, I would be alerted by more of these seemingly throwaway lines delivered in order to support his acquaintance with – occasionally his actual presence at – those occasions in other people's lives in which he could not possibly have been involved. Perhaps it was merely an affectation, discreetly, even subconsciously, forwarded, of a man who preferred to be stage-centre in any event under discussion.

I looked again at Mr Welldone's profile presented against the back-drop of chestnut trees to ascertain whether he had inherited any of the autocracy, not to say cruelty, of Gunner Jingo, his artilleryman forbear, not averse to roping mutineers in his regiment to the mouths of cannons, then giving the order to fire. A certain haughtiness about the eyes, to be expected from one now revealed as close, or supposedly close, to the throne, overlaid an otherwise kindly enough face that continued to suggest to me the physiognomy of those engravings of eighteenth-century composers seated at spinets whose powdered wigs conspire to conceal their age. Of course, this escapade in the queen's grounds might have been effected simply because Welldone knew one of the park keepers or gardeners on the royal estate. One thought not, though.

'I have some letters Gordon wrote to Strange. You might be interested in looking them over.'

'I'd be very keen to see them. I never knew they kept in touch.'

'I'll dig them out, then. They are in store in London.'

On the way back home, George asked me to swap places with him so that he could conduct an examination of the built-in gadgetry available to passengers in the back seat of Mr Welldone's Flying Spur. There were buttons to be pressed for adjusting the temperature and the lighting of the lavishly furnished interior, for opening and shutting the windows and for allowing the leather seats to fall backwards and electrically caress the passenger with a soothing massage. There was television to be watched, computer screens to be tapped, apertures to be slid open for an exploration of the contents, a refrigerator pillaged for food and drink for sustenance on this return journey, a detachable remote from which George could give Drake orders. George manipulated the car's stereo system through its multiple channels at varying, for the most part earsplitting, volumes. Mr Welldone took all this well.

George then spoke accusingly to our host.

'You know my aunt Yseult,' he said. He pronounced her name as he always did as Auntie Salt.

'I do,' Mr Welldone replied in the deepest voice he had yet assumed. He exhibited no surprise at this sudden question. 'She no longer visits, I understand.'

'We upset her.'

'What is she to you?'

'She's my grandma's cousin.'

'I had no idea there was any connection. Our paths crossed in London briefly only a month or two ago. I recall now, George, that you were with her. I was wondering where I had seen you before.'

'She called you "Master."'

'Did she? I'd forgotten.'

With this revelation that it was Mr Welldone before whom Yseult had knelt in the London art gallery, Drake had driven up to our front door. I prompted George to thank him for the ride, thanked him myself. I did not expect to see him again for a while unless, if he remembered his promise, he were to produce the Adam Lindsay Gordon letters. However, a small mishap brought us fortuitously together again only a day or so later.

Concerning the arrangements for the wedding of Guy and of Gwendoline, Ganson knew of 'a little man' who would hire out morning coats for the two of us at a tithe of the cost of any of our local outfitters. I was deputed to pick the stuff up. Ganson's contact was situated a fair distance away. George and I drove out there. The minor accident to the car, enough to halt us on our journey and leave us for a while stranded by the roadside, should not be ascribed to the argument that had broken out concerning the rules of the public-house cricket game undertaken on our journey. Divergence of opinion had centred on The Coach and Horses. It had been agreed that twenty runs should be added to George's team's score, a total dictated by the inn-sign's depiction of a coach and four, the horses' legs and the coachman's, together with his two arms, each counting as a single, a fairly massive total to have been yielded up by just one pub. That was not in dispute. For all that, my opinion was that the coach, being limbless, constituted a wicket. Here was the rub. George was adamant that the design should be considered as a whole and not separately, after the manner of another house passed earlier on, the Rose and Crown, which had counted as only one wicket, not two wickets, for his side then in the field.

'You should think yourself lucky, we couldn't see inside the coach,' George said. 'It could have been carrying passengers, say six, equals another twenty-four runs.'

'The coach was returning empty to a stable-block a few miles from an hotel where the passengers had alighted for their lunch.'

'Dad, I sometimes think you have no place in the real world. You should be giving lectures on fairy-stories instead of the poetry that nobody will ever read.'

'May I be allowed to continue? When the coach reaches the stable it will be given a thorough airing because of the fishy aroma of its interior. The passengers now at their oceanic luncheon table are octopuses. Eight of them. Had they been on board you would have added sixty-four runs to your score. You win some, you lose some, that's the way you have to look at it.'

George leaned back in his seat and struck out at the dashboard with a trainered foot.

Woke up this morning, answered the telephone:
You said, 'Meet me on the corner, have your black drawers on.

I could never be sure if it was the sudden burst of the woman's blues-inflected voice against a raucously blown saxophone accompaniment blaring from the car's sound system or the two dogs amiably squabbling (as were we) on the grass verge and threatening to run across our path that was the cause of our careering off the road and landing in a ditch.

We clambered out. Neither of us had suffered so much as a bruise, the front of the car bearing the brunt of the collision, its bonnet now embedded firmly in marshy earth. George slid down the bank and dabbled a foot in the ditch's brackish water.

'I suppose you wouldn't happen to have your mobile about you?'

'No,' George said. 'And I bet you haven't got yours.'

I hadn't. My dislike of mobile telephones did not extend to Ganson's but I had never succumbed to their usefulness other than to have one about me when George and I were apart. Today the gadget remained on the kitchen table.

'Right in one. We had better start walking.'

'Where to, dad?'

'Back home.'

'But it's miles.'

'Didn't we pass a garage a few minutes ago? They'll sort us out.'

We began the ascent of a steep hill. Before us the road rose, as George had said, for miles ahead. I thought of Christina Rossetti's poem:

> Does the road wind up-hill all the way?
> Yes, to the very end.
> Will the day's journey take the whole long day?
> From morn to night, my friend.

A couple of vans drove past us without stopping. We trudged on. The sun came out. It grew hotter. Then, ahead of us, a klaxon warned anybody with any sense to get out of the way of whoever was powering a machine to be seen a moment later cresting the rise at a fair speed. The sun's rays dancing on her bonnet blinded our sight as the car swooped upon us. The horn stopped braying. The car braked. The driver wound down the window of the Flying Spur.

'Hop in,' Drake said.

*

In the café next morning Drake took his lugubrious place. He had buttoned himself into a jacket heavily padded under his arms or at least

96

under his left arm that gave him the appearance of hunching up one shoulder to ward off a blow.

'Thanks for yesterday,' I said. 'The doughnuts are on me.'

'Ta muchly,' Drake said. 'What are you doing this morning?'

'Nothing.'

'You are now. I'm taking you to that tailor johnny you were meant to go to yesterday. His Nibs's orders. To tell the truth, the journey is a gobshagging nuisance. My nan will go spare if I'm late home for my tea.'

Drake's estimate of the inconvenience brought about by this new burst of his employer's generosity was fiercely expressed. That in itself was nothing new. Almost every order received by Drake was catalogued as tiresome in the extreme, adding to a workload already intolerably heavy and advancing by some months the hour of his resignation. That was what he cautioned. Threats were probably not to be taken seriously. Despite a formidable bulk proposing he should not be crossed and accentuated this morning by his bulging coat, there was an altogether softer, even a soppy, side to Drake after the manner of expectantly fierce dogs who, going for the throat, end up slobbering their victim with kisses.

He used his mobile to see about the car. For this particular expedition, long corroded mechanisms needed to be oiled before as he put it, 'this show could roll.' The protracted telephone call to the garage concerned transportation, whether the big limousine, the Flying Spur, should carry us to the tailor's or one of several smaller runabouts belonging to Drake's master might be more suited to the route – either a motorway or the back lanes and rolling hills on which George and I had been stranded – by which our journey was to be conducted.

Mr Welldone was again unexpectedly present. We had travelled some way when I thought I should point out to Drake that we were on the wrong road. Mr Welldone intervened. 'We are going to London first of all. I hope that does not put you to any inconvenience.' One was conscious in those few words, phrased with perfect courtesy, that one had been put in one's place.

We threaded our way through city traffic. Without exhibiting aggression or sounding his horn as he had so provocatively done on the hill where he picked George and me up yesterday Drake nosed a quietly authoritative path through the traffic. Memories returned of the pride I had felt as a boy when riding with Major and Mrs Scott in their similarly handsome Citroën DS19. Drake drew us to a halt in a street off Piccadilly.

We entered a large secondhand bookshop. Master and chauffeur made for the stairs leading to a basement section. I was struck as always when entering these places with the likelihood, devolving on occasion into certainty, that there would be nothing, however cheaply marked, that I would want to buy. This negative perspective was compatible with the general attitude to life itself experienced before my beloved son came to live with me, an anticipatory enthusiasm for something I was about to do instantly withdrawn the moment the event was set in motion. These days of course this indigenous gloom had been dissipated by the constant pleasure in George's companionship. In this shop melancholy stirred once more. There was an elusive tract on the Buckinghamshire village I was researching that might possibly be stocked here although it was with no real expectation of finding a copy that I went in search of it but rather to pass the time until Drake and Mr Welldone should be finished with their business downstairs.

Then I came across a copy of *So Much of the Diary of Lady Willoughby as Relates to her Domestic History, & to the Eventful Period of the Reign of Charles the First*. It was a find I had no intention of buying but I would report on its presence to my academy colleague, Scottie McLeod. We had compiled, or rather committed to memory, a list of some dozen or so books to be almost universally available in whichever secondhand bookshop we found ourselves, *If Winter Comes, Enter Three Witches* – as a boy interested in the occult this had turned out disappointing – *The Scallop*, a richly gilded quarto distributed gratis, so Scottie said, to all shareholders in Shell Oil, most of whom had jobbed them off for whatever price they could get, Max Müller's *Chips from a German Workshop*, several other titles besides. I wondered if a game could be devised where prizes were given for finding or, come to that, for failing to find these titles to which as I wandered round I found a possible addition to bookshop ubiquity in a leather-bound copy of Motley's *Dutch Republic*. McLeod might disallow its admission as occupying more than one volume. All the same, we might add a new section for sets of books, Motley, Prescott's *Spain*, any of John Galt's novels, John Brown's *Horae subsecivae*, the thirteen volumes of the Sanskrit fantasies of F. W. Bain.

Mr Welldone was taking his time. I was getting bored. I began a second tour of the shelves, alerted to the presence of a shop assistant at a desk who had every now and then produced a sharp barking cough and a scraping of his feet over the floorboards, the first that relayed a message that my every movement was under surveillance, the second that he found my presence irritating in the extreme. Seated alone in the shop when we came in and without raising his head from the papers engaging his attention, this man had offered no indication that we were welcome. Secondhand booksellers, antiquarians as they prefer to be called, are past masters at intimidation, chilling whatever pleasure a customer may be deriving from his visit by an ingrained hostility directed across their premises in icy blasting waves.

In a corner of the shop stocking modern, low-priced, books in their original jackets, I found a title overlooked in a second list maintained by McLeod. He held the opinion that books whose titles included a personal pronoun were to be avoided: to give some instances, *My Dog Tulip, Our Village, Aimez-vous Brahms?, As You Like It, We Didn't Mean to Go to Sea*. Here was a title he had missed: *They Asked for a Paper* by C. S. Lewis. I was looking to see if the marked price were cheap enough to warrant my getting it and presenting it to McLeod, when the member of staff on duty called my name.

'Saunders.'

Even though the assistant had recognized me, he did not look in my direction but kept his eyes focussed on the shop door as if anticipating the descent of yet more book-lovers to interrupt a morning's cataloguing. The profile seemed familiar. Still keeping his face turned sideways, he repeated my name.

'Saunders.'

'Amos.'

I had not seen him since schooldays when he was the leader of our table-turning clan, even at the age of thirteen well up on occult lore and brooking no flippancy in the course of our explorations into the world of spirit. Well after our Sunday séances had been abandoned, he had maintained his fascination for the supernatural and, some years later when he was in the sixth form, had been caught in a lesson studying beneath his desk a book of magical instruction, 'a grimoire of the blackest dye' the master who had discovered this tract observed. Amos had marked the names of two or three of the seventy-two mighty demons listed therein with their sigils and the appropriate summonses to be recited for their evocation to visible appearance. I reminded him of those days.

Amos fell silent. He turned further away from me as if to look for a title on a shelf running along the side of his bureau holding poetry books bound in polished calf, as a rule school prizes for English studies. These books, sold nowadays only for decoration, are always to be found in good condition since the titles were seldom the prize-winner's choice of reading but the school's principal's, selected as literature held to improve the mind. Southey would be among the books on offer, Longfellow, Scott, William Collins, Samuel Rogers. Adam Lindsay Gordon was another likely candidate.

Amos spoke again.

'I've abandoned all magical experimentation.'

'In disillusionment?'

'In fear. I burned my fingers. And my face.' He spun himself halfway round in his chair, presenting his opposite profile. No hair grew, would ever grow again, on the left side of his head. From the middle of his skull, down one cheek, and narrowly missing his left eye stretched a wide pale unevenly patched skin graft that ran below his collar line where his shirt may have covered a further extension of this terrible burn. 'A small psychic mishap. It taught me the age-old lesson that when you knock on the gates of heaven, it is the gates of hell that open first.'

'By ineluctable law.'

'So you know the quotation?'

'A relative of mine used it once.'

'You were lucky that old major of yours warned you off our Sunday séances. You should be eternally grateful to him.'

Amos swung back to present once again the unafflicted side of his face. 'What are you doing here?'

'I came in with Mr Welldone? He's picking up some manuscripts.'

'That is Count Rakozky.'

'His chauffeur calls him Welldone.'

'Really. How peculiar. Perhaps to protect his identity. He is very well connected.' Amos placed a finger to the unscarred side of his nose.

'To the point of driving his car at a hundred m.p.h. through a royal park.'

'I'm not surprised to hear that. I would advise you...'

Amos had no time to conclude whatever precept he had in mind to offer. Further conversation was interrupted by a violent opening of the shop door. A traffic warden stood there.

'That your car outside?' he asked me. 'It must be moved at once.'

Drake came thundering up the basement stairs. He placed his large bulk between me and the warden.

'Who says?'

'I say.'

Drake expanded muscles in preparation for any eventuality in this confrontation. A button detached itself from his constricting jacket. It fell rattling to the floor like a tossed coin. He pointed out in gruff tones that we had a dispensation. A pass was produced. The warden was unimpressed.

'Never seen one like that before.'

'No, you wouldn't of,' Drake said, 'because you are employed in too shit a position ever to have been shown one of this nature.'

'I'll need to take instruction.'

A walkie-talkie was employed. After a crackling exchange the warden gave a sharp salute. He left the shop.

'That's him fucked,' Drake said. He followed the warden out at the same time as Mr Welldone, apparently now to be thought of as Count Rakozky, came up the stairs. He carried a cardboard box.

'The Gordon letters you wanted to see. We'd better make tracks before Drake gets into any more trouble. Come along.'

I said a hasty goodbye to Amos. He bowed his head in understanding at the necessity for me to jump to the Count's command: if Count he were.

In the car, he asked how I knew the bookshop assistant. 'It's the first time I've seen him there,' he said. 'How did he come by that dreadful burn?'

How indeed? I wouldn't have asked Amos how the accident occurred – perhaps inflicted in anger at being summoned from his hellish abode by one of the seventy-two infernal spirits listed in the book of spells he had been intercepted reading at school – even if I'd had the time to make the enquiry. I gave some noncommittal answer. It puzzled me that the Count knew of Amos's disfigurement when, as he admitted, he had never seen him before and when Amos had been so particular about keeping the ruined side of his face hidden from his customers. Even if he had caught a glimpse of the scar reflected in the glass of a bookcase why, I asked myself, had the Count assumed it had been the result of a burn?

We now made for the country. Ganson's tailor was found to occupy the first floor of a building with a charity shop at street level. Welldone, now Racokzy, plunged in. 'A worthy cause. I'll put a pound in their collecting-box. Give me a call when you come out.'

Ganson had added a grey top hat to the frock coat and trousers he would be wearing for the wedding. I put it on and carried his other clothes and mine down the stairs.

'Very smart,' Mr Welldone said. 'I sometimes sport a topper. Ascot and such events. My gracious, whatever's been going on here?'

We had taken our places in the back seat of the car. Drake was not at the wheel. There was no sign of him in the street. It was odd he had left the doors unlocked. Some objects had been arranged on the driving seat, the pass that had absolved Drake from a parking fine outside the bookshop, the keys of the car, a pair of driving gloves. Among this array lay an automatic pistol. Its encasement within a shoulder holster explained Drake's seemingly contorted arm I had noted in the café before we had begun our journey. Its abandonment and its flagrant exposure to general view were unequivocal indications that Drake had jumped ship. Count Racozky had been deprived of his driver and, it was revealed, his bodyguard as well.

'Alas and alack,' the Count said, 'we've got a deserter on our hands. Or rather, out of our hands. He always said he'd walk out on me one day. I'm afraid Adam Lindsay Gordon was the straw that broke this particular camel's back.' Mr Welldone pointed to the pistol on the driver's seat.' Pass that thing over here, would you be so kind? I suppose there's no chance you can drive this machine?'

'I think I can. I learned to drive in a car much this size.'

'So you did,' Mr Welldone said abstractedly. He may have been considering how best to explain away Drake's abandoned weapon. He offered no further comment, but continued to express his pleasure at my being able to get us back to base. It was a pleasure to drive his powerful and responsive car. It reminded me yet again of my boyhood days when I had exulted in being allowed behind the wheel of Major Scott's *Déesse*. I avoided the temptation to 'open her up,' as Drake had put it, and negotiated the roads slowly and carefully, obeying finally Mr Welldone's request to drop him at our local garage.

'One of the mechanics here will ferry me home,' he said. 'Don't forget this.' He handed me over the box containing the A. L. Gordon letters.

I got in at about half past three. I debated whether or not to tell George I had been driving Mr Welldone's Flying Spur. He would be disappointed not to have been of the party. The spare hour before he came home from school could be spent reading the Gordon correspondence the Count had entrusted to me. I took off the lid of the shoe box which, as I carried it home, had struck me as rather heavy for a receptacle containing only a batch of old papers. Perhaps there were some books in it as well, the Count's ancestor, Gunner Jingo's, blood-and-thunder autobiography, for instance, that had been published in the eighteen-nineties and ran to over five hundred pages. There were no books in the box. Underneath the letters Mr Welldone had secreted Drake's automatic.

There seemed a touch of malice in what must have been done deliberately, presumably to rid himself of the responsibility of owning a weapon for which he may have had no licence. Here again one detected the high-handedness of the aristocrat. His behaviour all day had been odd, uncanny too in the way he had been aware of Amos's disfigurement when it had not been put on show and his knowing, or claiming he knew, that I had learned how to drive in a car the size of his own. I had no idea how to get in touch with him now that Drake had defected. That may have been his motive for asking to be let out of the car at the garage instead of allowing me to drive him to wherever it was he lived.

The pistol, almost certainly loaded – there would be little point in a bodyguard's carrying an unprimed weapon – had better be chucked into the river. For the time being, I put it in a place where George couldn't find it; and then, because events began to take a strange turn, I forgot about it.

CHAPTER VII

For some time, Molly had expressed herself as worried about Terence, reporting that he had been 'overdoing things.' His behaviour had grown distinctly odd, she said. He had been brought home by the police who had found him one night wandering around Oxford, a repetition of the incident when I had come across him locally. Again, he was at a loss to explain what he was doing in the city. There had also been some trouble in the public library where he had shouted things out, 'silly things' was all Molly would say about this outburst, and had to be forcibly removed. His preoccupation with the time of day had become ever more worrisome, eventually taking precedence over all other activities and leading to his being hospitalized as a victim of, in his own phrase, Old Timers' Disease. For a while Molly advised me not to go and see him, but George, who missed his grandfather, kept urging me to make a visit to ensure he was being well looked after and fit enough for George to come and say hello.

A receptionist gave me a cup of coffee and pointed me in the direction of the visitors' room. A glass skylight illuminated a round table strewn with colour supplements from newspapers immemorially outdated. Around the walls on which were papered notices of meal-times and admonitions against smoking were set hard wooden chairs. One corner was stacked with a pile of children's toys. Here Terence was kneeling in front of a miniature construction of ambiguous utility. He looked well enough, though somewhat knocked about.

'Wotcha,' he said, without getting up. 'Welcome to Bedside Manor. I was beginning to think you weren't coming. What time is it? This here puzzle runs on batteries. It's more difficult than it looks. The idea is, you catch hold of this bottle-opener thing and manoeuvre it slowly along this cable without touching it though, until you get to the top when a bell – bollocks – a bell will ring to announce the success of your enterprise. I have made – turds – friends with the one of the inhabitants of this place. He'll be down in a moment for his tea which is taken at exactly five minutes to four. Is it five to four yet? By the way, you couldn't lend me your watch, could you? They've taken mine away to be repaired. It'll be a few more days apparently. Go and sit down. I'll be finished here in a tick. Just got to work round a few more curves and then the bell – oh, bums.'

Terence's outbursts of temper were provoked by a buzzer that had been built into the interior of the puzzle contraption, setting itself off on a fairly regular basis, and signalling, as Terence explained, that his metal lever had touched the wire as he was negotiating its configurations, each time compelling the player to begin the whole endeavour anew. I pulled one of the chairs up to the table and opened a magazine at an article on caravanning. As I flicked through the pages wondering if George might enjoy a camping expedition and how difficult it might be to drive the car with a trailer attached, the waiting-room door was thrown back on its hinges. Another patient came in. He was in a wheelchair. His jaws were clamped on a lighted cigar, in disobedience, most likely deliberate disobedience, to the No Smoking signs papering this room. He dropped the cigar into my coffee saucer and propelled himself at full tilt across the floor. Using his feet as buffers he brought himself to a violent halt against the far wall.

'Visitors, Terence, visitors, or another one of your psycho-johnnies?'

'This here man, Dolorot, is my son-in-law, Drain'ole Saunders.'

Terence was employing his old trick of pronouncing people's names backwards. I tried to work out how 'Dolorot' would be pronounced the right way round.

'I once knew a Saunders. Dead, now, probably. Like everybody else.' The incapacitated man was a good age, well over eighty, I thought, alert enough in a birdlike, possibly hawkish, way, but a hawk unsure onto which next tree – or vole – to attach his claws. No wonder most of his friends were dead.

'You are a lucky man, Terence. I never have visitors. Nobody ever comes to see me.'

'Nonsense, Dolorot. Your step-daughter came only two days ago. In the morning. It was just gone the quarter past eleven, or so she said. What's the betting you can't remember her name.'

'That's where you're wrong. She's called Nosy Posy. And I'll tell you a secret. She's not my step-daughter because I never married her mother. I never would have married her mother. I would never have married anyone, never did. We were a good team though, her and me. She ministered to my needs. That daughter of hers is a cold fish, though. Glad when she took herself off. Let's all go outside. I want to finish my cigar.'

'You two go, I'll follow when I've cracked this little toy.' Terence turned back to his machine, but speaking over his shoulder asked after George.

'Is he still magicking?'

'Yes, most enthusiastically. He was keen to perform to grown-ups at a local wedding we're to celebrate, table-hopping as it's called. We managed to persuade him it was not the right occasion to make his adult debut.'

'Has he still got that magic coach?'

'Kit? Oh, yes. He's practically family.'

'He won't have him for long.'

'Why do you say that?'

'Because he will turn into a pumpkin.'

This was more like the old Terence. Despite his crawling about on hands and knees and engaging himself with children's toys that proposed a possible mental regression, Terence appeared to be behaving rationally enough. He asked about the wedding.

'Anyone we know?'

'No. Well, the bride, Gwendoline Holmes, is a student of mine. She's marrying a rich local brewer, Guy, Sir Guy, actually, Sir Guy Wendon.'

'Um.' The buzzer went off again, stymying Terence's progress. It did not disturb his line of thought. 'Gwendoline Wendon. She'll be known as Gwen Wen.'

'Ganson said as much. He's been putting his oar in, in a big way. He's hoping for some endowment for the academy in return for financing the wedding feast.'

The ancient in the chair broke in. He had wheeled himself up close to where I was sitting and had been listening attentively to what Terence and I had been saying. He was chuckling and muttering to himself the names 'Gwendoline, Guy.' Now, he began to spout poetry.

> Three weeks I slept at St Hubert's Chase;
> When I woke from the fever of wounds and wine
> I could scarce believe that the ghastly face
> That the glass reflected was really mine.
> I sought the hall where a wedding had been –
> The wedding of Guy and of Gwendoline.

He caught my arm as he spoke Adam Lindsay Gordon's lines. He wore a signet ring of hot metal, of steel heated to blistering point, that burned into my wrist. I made to tear myself away from this cauterising branding iron whose properties changed instantaneously from the

106

searingly hot to the bitingly cold. Then, instinctively, I gave up resistance in any form. I'd surrendered to that beringed hand before, long in the past. In those days, I was expected not to sing out, not to flinch, not to ask what was the motive behind that urgent grasp. Pressure would then be released and a whistle of pleasure would issue from a mouth of imperfect teeth.

Here, back from the dead, was Major Scott, Thorold, as I had once and only once heard his wife address him, 'Dolorot' in Terence's retrograde vocabulary, donor of my copy of Gordon's collected poetry with its healthful inscription exhorting me 'to run, to ride, to swim': not in fact to waste my boyhood in the darkened séance-room I was inhabiting when we first met. I was never able to ask him when, as a boy sitting next to him in the back seat of his car, from what icy metal his finger-ring had been constituted. To have spoken of it within earshot of his wife who was nosing us dutifully along on our Sunday afternoon outings would have exposed the procedure occasioning the contact that, I recalled, I used to liken to a doctor's needle injected at regular appointments so that over time apprehension had been succeeded by tolerance, and, finally, by connivance as the treatments began to occasion wellbeing.

'Thorold?' I had never before called him by his first name.

'Of all people.' The Major looked up from his chair and shyly smiled. Gone were the projecting teeth and in their place was exhibited an ivory bridgework of a perfect, if unambiguously false, alignment. His moustache, of no further benefit for disguising the protruding originals, had been shaved off and the leg that his wife used to say occasionally 'gave him gyp' had now consigned him to immobility.

'And you are Leonard. Leonard Saunders. Prince of the ectoplasm. Did you ever get the money?'

'Money?'

'Some money I sent you. Years ago now. Rude of me to ask, really. It was meant to tide you over your university years, add a bit more comfort than your father could have provided. Army officers aren't especially well paid or they weren't in my day.'

'Was it a large sum of money? A very large one?'

'Not compared with the value of your friendship. You see, being the sort of person I am, after you went and grew up on me, I…'

Major Scott's reply was cut short by a fit of coughing.

All this time, the smoke from his Havana that lay smouldering in the saucer had been producing a more pungent, far less fragrant, aroma than might be expected from a seriously expensive cigar. Terence began to choke. The air grew ever thicker, more acrid. Then licks of flame and a crackle of newsprint arose from the table where the colour supplements had been spread out. The Major's cigar had fallen out of my coffee saucer and had set the papers on fire.

Almost immediately, a piercingly shrill alarm went off, activating a flurry of activity. Various members of staff, some in white coats, hurried in. A nurse whose starched uniform echoed the crackling of the bonfire on the table wheeled Major Scott sharply out of the room, a porter activated a fire extinguisher. The siren screamed on.

Terence had vanished. I stood alone in the smoke-filled room. An executive in a dark suit came in. Over the noise of the alarm, he listened to my shouted explanation of events in which, while absolving myself from causing the accident, I refrained from naming Major Scott as the culprit. He thought it better that I cut short my visit to my father-in-law and returned another day. That would be my best plan. The receptionist at the entrance would arrange a suitable date, he said. She was at her desk now if I cared to go along straight away.

Much more had needed saying.

CHAPTER VIII

Some days later the doorbell rang. I was expecting Ganson who wanted to discuss the wedding plans which, despite some reservations of Colin Bailey's, were well advanced. I buzzed him in.

A woman came up the stairs. Her slim figure was set off by a coat and trousers suit of leaf-green cloth. The garment drew attention to what had to be put down as a 'good' figure, at the same time announcing in the masculinity of its cut that the wearer was to be conceived of as in fighting trim. She was tall but not as tall as she might have liked to be. Extra height had been imparted by a pair of high-heeled shoes. She wore a choker of green stones set in metal around a long enquiring neck, above which her facial expression was one of controlled concern, as if somebody, although certainly not herself, were in need of the support that she and she alone would be able to provide. A straight haircut allowed a longish fringe to fall over one side of her forehead, imparting a look of considerable slyness. She toted a large bag of recyclable material from which she produced a printed card. It read: 'Professor Roz Hathaway. Humanistic and Cognitive Behaviour Therapist. Private Counselling by Appointment.'

'You are George's father? Good. I'm glad to have caught you at home. We need to speak about your son.'

I had no idea who this woman was or how she knew George's name. I was certain she hadn't been sent by his school. Percy, as he called his headmaster, occasionally telephoned to resolve some minor misdemeanour justified by George as having parental sanction, these calls always ending on an affable note. He had in fact rung up last week to ask me to persuade George to join the choir. 'Active fellows like George sometimes feel it is a bit pansy to be a chorister. It's the cassock I suppose, that sort of thing; but his music master says he has perfect pitch.'

'Unlike his leg breaks.'

Percy laughed heartily. 'Call in for a noggin next time you're round this way. I wish all my fathers were like you.'

Professor Hathaway had seated herself at a table and drawn from her bag a plastic bottle of water. She unscrewed the top and drank deeply from the contents. She looked towards me as if to suggest that her determinable physical fitness could never be mine until such time as this dietary supplement were adopted by myself as well, although for sanitary considerations she felt unable to pass the bottle across. She opened our discussion.

'We need to talk about George's attitude problem.'

'Do we?'

'Does the child exhibit any form of mood disorders within the home environment?'

'He is his father's despair. He spits out his food, he smashes glasses, he throws his toys out of the window, he strangles kittens, and he's been known to threaten me with a violent death if I ever suggest he might think of attending school on anything that could be called a regular basis. You'll forgive me, Miss Hathaway, if I ask you who the hell you are and what business it is of yours?'

The Professor allowed herself a thin smile, a smile that spoke more of compassion for the man who had resorted to humour than for its diverting effect on the listener. It was immediately withdrawn. She made another call on her bottle and brushed aside her boyish fringe of hair. Her verdant suiting gave her the look of a not unimposing Robin Hood, but a Robin Hood whose personality had been overlaid with an uncharacteristic sourness. She was not to be accounted the jaunty outlaw of pantomime tradition but a strategist of infinite cunning, an androgynous, or nearly androgynous, dodger behind the greenwood trees, bow and arrow at the ready to snipe at her foes: at the Baron's men or at her own band it mattered not once they had got in her way. Whether, when this role-playing came to an end, when as Ganson put it, the shades lengthen and the evening comes, she would wish to turn up the volume of her womanhood trailed in business hours only by the painted fingernails and the high heels (of which Molly would have sternly disapproved when worn with trousers) was open to question. The feeling was that she would not: that she would look upon any man who found her desirable with the same compassionate eye she focussed upon those referred to her for treatment. That seemed what she had in mind: to appear before her patients as an epicene figure blent with the leaves of the forest where she made her home and, instead of the gold and silver of the philanthropist of Nottingham's depredations, to offer the relief from mental stress that she was in a position to dispense. I clearly fell into this category.

'I will come to the point. It concerns a letter written to Oo May

Fashions whom I represent. I believe you wrote it.'

'My son wrote a letter to Oo May Fashions.'

'Indeed.' The Professor allowed herself another small smile of indulgence.

What I said was almost the truth. I had corrected George's spelling of 'spelling' and now gave thought to whether the Professor with her psychological expertise could explain his antipathy to the use of double consonants. I had recommended the erasure of a sentence I thought a touch over-menacing: added a comma here and there: provided the envelope: paid for the stamp. That was all.

It was Molly who had first brought his attention to this particular piece of insidious marketing. 'I don't think children should be dressed up like sandwich-board men. Am I right or am I wrong?'

It was never a good idea to say that Molly was wrong. Lips could be tightened, teacup carried to another room. In any case, this particular matter had my wholehearted approval. George, who had up to then been looking as if he had urgent business somewhere else, had set to work.

His idea had been to write to this children's clothing company whose trademark was sewn boldly onto the fronts of their hooded garments and present it with an ultimatum. No longer was he, nor the letter predicted, were several of his school friends, prepared to walk the streets blazoning across their chests the name of the outfitter whose clothes they wore when there was no financial reward on offer for these promotional services. George's fee for continuing to advertise the firm, his friends' too most likely when he had signed them up, was estimated at what he called an economic honorarium (both words properly spelt) of fifty pounds per calendar month payable in advance from the date at the head of his letter. Were this very fair request not to be granted, persuasive methods were at hand. Either the stitched-on letters spelling – *speling*, in George's individual style – the name of the firm would be unpicked from the wearers' chests and discarded or, giving less trouble, the jackets would be worn inside out. George had signed off by saying he felt there was no need to emphasize the catastrophic effect on the company's business if his treaty were overlooked.

His letter was intended to have been sent as an email. However, his grandmother's ignorance of computers, Terence's too, despite his cleverness with electrical circuiting, had encouraged George to use pen and ink far more often than his contemporaries. I asked Professor Hathaway whether she worked for the firm.

'I represent the company from time to time in my role as counsellor. I am consulted on the wording of intergenerational correspondence in order that the firm can empathise with the mindset of the kid who has communicated and elect as to how a reply should be toned. We do not relish interventionism but in this particular matter it must be apparent to you this is an issue that needs to be robustly addressed. Now you have told me that you were party to it I may mention that I hardly expected to have to counsel a male parent not to encourage his child to indulge in inappropriate behaviour towards a major retailing outlet such as Oo May. I'm sure his mother...'

'His mother is dead.'

For a moment the Professor was taken off guard. She regained her poise by means of a pull at her water. 'I'm sorry. As I was saying, it is of concern to us that a demand such as this could be posted on the internet by the child responsible and then go viral. Preferring not to commission a lawyer's letter requesting the writer to cease and desist, my superiors delegated me to initiate a parental dialogue and...'

'Fire a warning shot across daddy's bows. I'm sorry to disagree with you but I looked upon my son's idea as a rather pioneering move, striking out for the underdog, that sort of thing.'

'Imagine if every kid in the country asked for the same sort of reimbursement your child is hoping to extract from us.'

'I am imagining. Which is why I encouraged my son to go ahead. It demonstrates to Oo May that all they are good for is to manufacture serviceable garments to clothe a junior population. Then they can take advertisements in the national press announcing a reduction in price resulting from the needlessness any longer to embroider their clothes with their trademark. Or, to consider things from another angle, if you can't make your clothes recognizable by their superior quality alone, you might consider going out of business. How about that?'

'It is disappointing that you interpret it in that vein.'

'Furthermore, if you were to examine the affair from the point of view of a woman such as yourself given to good works, would you not say that the recruitment of children to parade themselves in public in furtherance of a firm's greater profit margin might be likened to sending little boys up chimneys? Why not just buy my son off with a ten-

112

pound-note? That's probably all he's after. Or would that be considered as pandering to a blackmailer?'

Before she could give an answer to this, the bell rang again. I admitted Ganson. He smelled, as always, of green peppers. There was no need to introduce him to the Professor. He knew her already: knew her well.

'Odds bodkins. Mona Abecassis, as I live and breathe. I haven't seen you in ages, simply ages. Are you keeping well? You look a bit pale and irregular.'

'I'm good, thank you.' The Professor spoke coldly. She did not seem at all pleased to see Ganson regardless, as he had observed, of the long interval elapsing since their last meeting.

'I didn't ask what you were, I asked how you were. What's your line these days, Mona, you fickle old thing? Still writing your household hints column? I never see our local paper now we have to pay for it.'

'I never wrote on household hints. I edited a self-help column.' The Professor may have felt it necessary to censor any mention of a past career not embracing a background of psychotherapy. Ganson was not going to allow this to pass without comment.

'It couldn't have been self-help. Unless of course you were answering your own questions. Which we must enter as a possibility, knowing as we do the wiles of the world of journalism.

> You cannot hope to bribe or twist
> Thank God, the British journalist.
> But knowing what the man will do
> Unbribed, there is no reason to.'

Ganson's banter, not to say rudeness, could, I saw, be turned to my advantage. I couldn't be half as rude to Hathaway as Ganson was being but if I told him what she was doing here it would be bound to elicit another torrent of abuse. I began to explain to Ganson the purpose of her visit. I was interrupted.

'I'd prefer you not to discuss our business with other parties.'

'Is the matter *sub judice*?'

'Pardon?'

'Have legal proceedings been initiated?'

'Ideationally it is our hope it will not come to that.' Ganson had made her uneasy. It was time she made her getaway. She took a last draught from her water bottle. Ganson broke into song:

Hey, hey, Mona,
Ooh-ooh, Mona.
Can you come out on the front?
Listen to my heart go bumpity-bump.

The Professor paid no attention to this serenade. She thrust her bottle back into her bag.

'We have moved forward as far as we can at this moment in time. I will leave you now. I may say to my superiors, may I not, that you will address the issue within a viable time-frame?'

'Mona, O best-beloved,' Ganson shouted down to the Professor as she clattered down the stairs, 'You can address an envelope, you can address an assembly, you can address a golf ball. But you cannot address an issue.'

I had found this woman insufferable. I reflected again on what sort of society she mixed in when she was off-duty. None. That was the answer. No-one in his right mind could feel at ease confronted with that self-consciously benevolent beanstalk of a woman: but then she didn't deal with people in their right mind.

'What a stupid thing she is. What did she tell you her name was?'

'Her visiting card said Professor Hathaway.'

'Professor, forsooth. And her name isn't Hathaway. She adopted that in the hope everyone'd think she was descended from Shakespeare's missus. Her mother kept a brothel for a bit, got busted, then fell in with some retired colonel of militia and became his *procureuse*. The daughter, Mona Rosamund, was briefly married to a Greek harbour-master. Name of Abecassis. Unlike Jackie Kennedy, Hathers wasn't seductive enough to capture a shipowner.'

'Wasn't there an indecent joke about a harbour-master?'

'Yes. Urchin on the quayside at Alexandria, "You want nice girl, nice boy, saucy postcards?" Angry ship's captain, "I want the harbour-master." Urchin, "It can be arranged." Mona's marriage didn't take. Her maiden name is Drayne, or Potts, or Pails, or Sink: something, anyway, to do with the washing-up.'

'You have got it in for her. Where did you meet?'

Ganson didn't answer that. Despite his invective, it was clear that he found the Professor of considerable allure. It is often the case that a man will speak lightly of a woman to whom he is attracted. I suspected that Ganson was trying to allay any such suspicion now that he had heard it was likely she and I would be in touch at a future date. It was debatable if the attraction were mutual. Perhaps it once had been: the spark thought susceptible of re-ignition. The Professor might be persuaded to relax a little in the company of a man who had no truck with her professional skills, over a stiff drink brushing her sly fringe of hair away from her right eye and confessing that her daytime job was, in Colin Bailey's phrase, 'a lot of old madam.'

Ganson came to the point. 'I wanted to have a word about the wedding of Guy and of Gwendoline.'

> 'I sought the hall where a wedding had been,
> The wedding of Guy and of Gwendoline.'

'Slids,Leonard, whatever are you talking about?'

'Adam Lindsay Gordon, *The Romance of Britomarte.* The poem is set in the times of the Commonwealth where Ralph Leigh, a rude and a reckless youth, has promised ...'

'Never mind about that now. This is important. Stairs and I have done a deal with Madam Tumbleova and for a fee yet to be finally negotiated she'll let us have her dance hall for the wedding breakfast. The happy couple's table will be laid on the stage from where the speeches will be delivered. All other guests will be accommodated in the auditorium. Stairs has requisitioned tables and benches from the church hall. No charge, the verger johnny there said, provided he got an invitation. How's that for freeloading? There'll have to be champagne of course, though only for the toasts, I think. Stairs is of the opinion we can probably get away with...You're not listening, are you?'

I wasn't. I was thinking of reporting to Ganson what had been pre-occupying me ever since my visit to the care home, confiding in him the source of the improbable windfall of twenty years ago and my friendship with the man who must now be called my benefactor and who had introduced me to Gordon's poetry. Now I knew that the money had always been legally mine my conscience should have been clear. Major Scott had made it plain that my stint at his helm had been terminated not because he thought me diseased, subjected to the *foetor* that would attack me if I continued to dabble in the occult, but because I had become too old for a man of his tastes. That fact had never occurred to me, even though I suppose I had accepted that his actions were of a experimental nature – a prelude only to what I was already conceiving as the 'real thing' – from which he had never managed to extricate himself.

I ought to have told him at the home how grateful I was that, with his present of my smart and valuable racing bicycle, he had done me a good turn by rescuing me from the seedy world of table-turning and its likely descent into the sorceries from which Amos had been so terribly disfigured and had shoved me, as a schoolfellow might shove a friend into the exhilarating waters of a cold swimming-bath, back into the decencies of boyhood, into the 'nimbleness and lightness of limb' extolled by the poet whose words he had inscribed in my copy of Gordon's collected poetry. That such a person should have shaped my future might put me in a bad light with Ganson who could conclude or, knowing him, tell me to my face that I had alluringly milked this man of a good deal of money. I apologised for being inattentive. Ganson nodded his head.

'As I was saying...'

CHAPTER IX

On the morning of the wedding, George was in poor temper. He sat at breakfast kicking his heels against the legs of his chair. He was reading an old book he'd found when Cyrus and he had raided the loft.

'What's happening?'

'What? Oh, basically, they've set sail for the island. The sea's very rough. Sills has been sick in a bucket. His face was green and shining with sweat. I bet there'll be a band.'

'On the island?'

'At your wedding party. There'll be a band with a woman caterwailing. They'd have done better to have a magician, basically.'

'Better and quieter. And cheaper.'

'Not necessarily. What's for breakfast?'

'A kipper.'

'Yom kippur.'

'Yom kippur has a lean and hungry look. Would he were fatter.'

'You are quoting again.'

'Yes, afraid so.'

'Who from?'

'Shakespeare. *Julius Caesar*, Act One, Scene Two. Caesar on Cassius.'

'How do you know it's a he?'

'What is a he?'

'The kipper. The fatter kipper. Do kippers do it?'

'What?'

'You know. It.'

'Oh, It. No. Yes. In a way. Eggs, roe. That way.'

'There are lots and lots of ways of doing It, aren't there, basically?'

'Patterns vary, for sure.'

'And It doesn't always have to be for making babies either, does it?'

'Not necessarily.'

'And you don't have to love the person or not specially. There's two sorts of love, I'd say, love and love and love and It.'

At that hour of the morning and with a long day ahead, it would have been foolhardy to enter a debate on a Platonic ethic for which, with all the time in the world, I would be unable to offer any cut and dried solution, let alone one that would stand George in good stead if, as was unlikely, he would remember what he had been advised.

117

'People look at that question in different lights.'

'Suppose they would, basically.' George got up and hauled himself into his school bag. 'I'm off, dad. And before you ask, yes, I have got my sensible shoes on.'

'Basically.'

'That's not funny.'

'It's funny a bit.'

'It's not funny lots. Bye, dad. Love you.'

I cleared George's plate. He had performed a neat, almost a surgical, operation on his kipper in opposition to my inability to dissect his question on sexual morality. I changed into the hired tail-coat and went down to the café. Ganson strode in, egg-head shining, beard manicured, ratatouille redolences at a minimum. He'd rung me up the night before to ask if we could meet before the wedding. 'Just a private word over coffee before the proceedings kick in. I might down a strengthening slug of brandy if they serve it so early in the day.' He placed his top hat carefully on the floor beside his chair.

'That's what gentlemen did in Proust's time,' he observed, 'when they went visiting.'

'What are you talking about?'

'Society in the *Belle Epoque*. When gentlemen went visiting they put their top hats by the side of their chairs.'

'That way up?'

'God's wounds, what a pedant you are. You'll find the reference in *Le côté des Guermantes*.'

'On the subject of Proust, that topper makes you look a bit like Charles Swann.'

'Do you think so? Swann, you'll recall, was a man of a certain position in society.'

'That's what I mean.'

'Well, thank you. I confess I've been to some trouble to tidy myself up for this event. How's George?'

'Packed off to school. Reluctantly. He'd hoped I'd invite him to come along and do some table-hopping: a few card tricks, some fire-eating with candles he's just learned.'

Ganson plucked at his newly-trimmed beard. Despite a Proustian exterior, he seemed ill at ease. Doubtless he was concerned that the day, or his part of it, should go without a hitch. He drank off his brandy.

'I hope the service won't go on too long.'

'I'm going to skip it.'

'A pity. There's always such a lot to do in church. Read the memorial tablets, ogle the deaconess – or the choirboys if you're that way inclined – add, subtract, divide, multiply the numbers on the hymn-board until you arrive at a cabalistically significant figure (that's what old Amos would have done, isn't it?), count how many times in his sermon the preacher says "as such," turn up in the *Book of Common Prayer* the 'Commination or Denouncing of God's Anger and Judgements against Sinners' which is strong enough meat to direct your attention back to the God in whose temple you find yourself, to use your redoubtable cousin's phrase, if you don't want Him to cast you into eternal darkness. Still, if you won't, you won't. Now, a final word about the wedding breakfast. You and I have been placed next to each other. Rosamund Hathaway will be on your other side.'

So this was what Ganson had to impart. No wonder he had been obliged to work up slowly to a revelation threatening to ruin a day never in the first place likely to be of any very marked amusement. The news merited the need for a steadying glass of brandy on my part rather than on Ganson's. I wondered how he had managed to wangle an invitation for this tiresome woman of whom, despite his animadversions on almost all her characteristics, it was now clear he was in relentless pursuit. He attempted some propitiation for an act he saw at once I found disagreeable.

'She's not such a bad old frump when you get to know her.'

We swung our legs over wooden benches facing rough trestle tables reminding me of Gordon's *Britomarte* where the wedding of Guy and of Gwendoline was celebrated in the great hall of St Hubert's Chase. I looked around the assembly to see if I could find a face that would fit the part of the grizzled trooper who, years on, was still professing his love for the bride over an evening of steady drinking with his comrades. Kemp had been in love with Gwendoline since they were childhood playmates: any kind of a love affair was out of the question. These thoughts diverted me, uncivilly, from greeting Roz Hathaway who, sensing the waves of dislike which wafted towards her as strongly as Ganson's more peppery effusions, had been studiously engaging the guest on her right. She made a pretence of being surprised to find me on her other side.

'How are you?'

'Still of the same mind.'

The Professor gave one of her indulgent smiles. 'We won't talk about the letter issue now and spoil a fun day.' She leaned across me to enquire after a friend of Ganson's who had been unwell, taking on as she did so the same look of concern she had adopted at our interview, a burden that was not permitted to overload a shield of embodied toughness when engaged with other people's misfortunes. Like Ganson, she'd done herself up a bit, carmined her lips, added a touch of mascara beneath the slanting eyes. The Robin Hood suiting had been discarded for a pair of bell-bottomed silk trousers and a jacket of silver brocade. The glimpse of a white bodice worn next to the skin offered an allurement forborne in the Sherwood Forester get-up of our first meeting.

Wine and food arrived. Ganson commandeered a bottle of claret for personal consumption. 'I know we're having fish but I've never been able to drink white wine, regardless of its vintage. Tastes like a tart's widdle.' He said this quite loudly.

A small man, serviceably dressed as a minor church functionary, offered a hand across the table.

'Ta for the invite. Hawley Fawcett. Call me Hawley.'

Ganson turned to me and put a hand over his mouth. '"If you're waking call me Hawley. Call me Hawley, mother dear."'

'I am the one who's meant to do the quotations.'

'I didn't think anybody had been called Hawley since Dr Crippen.'

Fawcett probably heard Ganson's aside. He was not to be deflected by the murderous association. There was something he needed to relate, something, he predicted to Ganson, that would be bound to raise a chuckle. He set about recalling the incident, seen on television in the course of a programme concerning the manufacture and worldwide distribution of peanut butter. The anecdote took some time to draw to its close.

'I still laugh about it now.' Fawcett smiled round at us for ratification that the anecdote owned to comicality enough to sustain repeated tellings. A brief silence fell. Then Hawley asked Ganson, 'Are you partial to peanut butter?'

This was too much for Ganson, up to that point busy with his plate of salmon and cucumber salad. He swallowed a glass of his wine and shot Fawcett a look of pure hatred.

'I am about as partial to peanut butter as I am to Zyklon B.'

Hawley took this well. He fumbled in his cassock pocket for a tissue to stifle his laughter. A three-piece band struck up. A woman in a sequined evening gown began a song.

> The girl that I marry will have to be
> As soft and as pink as a nursery.

Here was George's predicted chanteuse. She didn't caterwaul as George had suggested she might but her voice and the accompanying music were loud enough to inhibit conversation. We got on with the salmon. Suddenly Ganson gave a cry.

'*Sapristi.*'

He had tipped a glass of his claret over the pale grey waistcoat of his morning clothes. He got to his feet and stared down at the damage. His beard was flecked with dashes of mayonnaise: 'all dappled with flakes of white foam,' as Gordon in his steeple-chasing poem had written of a racehorse's muzzle. He may have been drinking too deeply – that would have earned Gordon's Corporal Kemp's approval – wine taken in the daytime to which he had said he was unused on top of the early draught of brandy affecting co-ordination, or again, caught the sleeve of his tail-coat on the splintered edge of the table as he was pouring from his bottle.

'I must get you to put this into your washing machine the minute we're finished here' he said to me, 'or those tailor people will be charging me extra money.'

'I haven't got a washing machine.'

'*Saperlipopette*, Leonard, you're as much good as a sick headache. Have you got a washing machine, Mona?'

The Professor neither affirmed nor denied her ownership of a washing machine for the reason that she was categorically unable to recommend the remedy Ganson had in mind.

'On no account put the garment into a machine.' She spoke with some authority, most likely drawing on the rich archive of household tips deployed during her stint on the local newspaper. She gave as her opinion that there was only one sure-fire method to get rid of the wine stain: the waistcoat must be removed at once, laid upon a flat surface and the stained area liberally sprinkled with iced water – preferably soda water – and sea salt.

Ganson refused to have anything to do with a procedure of this kind.

'If you think I'm going to take off all my clothes and appear bollock naked in front of a distinguished wedding assembly, Mona, you must think again.' He sat down.

The Professor shrugged her brocaded shoulders and turned to me. 'Is it really true you haven't got a washing machine? We must see if we can't address the issue.' She offered one of her sly smiles.

Soon, the music stopped, plates were cleared, slabs of wedding cake set before us. When no-one was looking, I'd wrap my slice up and take it home for George. Hawley Fawcett left his alone too.

'I've always been in two minds about marzipan,' he said.

Some small children in blue velveteen trousers sped behind our chairs, shouting and waving coloured balloons.

'Kids love weddings,' Professor Hathaway remarked.

Ganson heard what she said. 'Kids.' Ganson shouted the word. 'Kids. I take you to mean children. Please do them the honour of referring to them as human beings. Kids are baby goats, that's what kids are. Kids have their throats cut on sacrificial altar-tops, kids are seethed in their mother's milk, kids are roasted whole on spits. That's what happens to kids. How would you like it if your children, not that you have any or are likely to, turned up at breakfast each morning, sat down, poured out their cornflakes and said to you and your husband, not that you have one or are likely to, "Good morning, goats." You wouldn't like it at all, would you? Have the courtesy, then, not to demean children who provide a more or less agreeable echelon of society. With the exception of this lot at our rear who are, as you have for once rightly observed, bestially constituted.'

'There's no call for unpleasantness,' the Professor said. 'And I'd prefer it if you didn't smoke.'

'"The Lord,"' Ganson replied, '"hath created medicines out of the earth and he that is wise will not abhor them." *Ecclesiasticus*, thirty-eight, four.'

Ganson dragged on his cigarette. He seemed to have forgotten about the damaged waistcoat. It was now apparent that his disobedience to his own commandment of not drinking until nightfall was resulting in this, even for him, excessive, incivility, the brandy in the café and the red wine, such of it as had not cascaded over him, irritating a compulsion now proving unconquerable. He needed to be quietened down if this breakfast were to go on for much longer. An adult voice was heard above the din, calling for silence. The children behind us obediently hushed one another, managing to make as much noise as before we had been called to order. A man rose to propose the health of the bride and groom. This man was Kit Buller. I was glad to see a friendly face.

When the speeches were over, the musicians struck up for a second time. The vocalist launched into another song from her repertoire commendatory of the marriage state. She held a glass of champagne that may have helped her in an aim for higher octaves. I would now be able to report to George that, as he had predicted, the singer was a caterwauler:

> Well I can see her now in her tight blue jeans
> Pumping all her money in the record machine
> Spinning like a top you should have seen her go
> I knew the bride when she used to rock and roll.

Sir Guy and Lady Gwendoline led some guests into the dance. Others were getting up from their seats, moving about, collecting stray page-boys, settling hats. Kit came over.

'Splendid to see you. How did you get here?'

'On a slight acquaintance with the bride. She is in my poetry class. Oh, and my boss laid on this do. I could ask you the same question.'

'Childhood mate of the groom. We used to sing in the same choir.'

'I forgot you sang.'

'Who are you?' Ganson was pointing a finger at Kit. For a few minutes he had been sitting, hiccupping quietly, crumbling his slice of cake between his fingers. Now he was on his feet. He did not wait for Kit to remind him how they had met but turned again to the Professor. I hoped he was not going to ask her to dance. Probably she wouldn't know how. If she danced at all, movements would likely be of a psychologically remedial nature only, the eurhythmics of Rudolf Steiner and his anthroposophical school of thought. She would do well to refuse. Ganson was now horribly drunk. The full extent of the damage to his waistcoat was exposed. He looked as if he had been shot in the stomach with an expanding bullet. He laid a hand on my shoulder to steady himself and addressed Hawley Fawcett across the table.

'I am going home now, sir, to lie between the thighs of a fat woman. And I assert and aver, they steam, sir, veritably steam.' He pointed himself towards the door and slowly jostled his way among the dancers as if, as the odd man out in a complicated cotillion, it would be his duty when his passage across the floor had been completed to salute a suitable lady whose partner would yield her into his arms and himself take over Ganson's orphaned and undulating place in the measure. He made it to the door, opened it, lurched into the daylight. Hawley was unaffected by Ganson's frank submission of his plans for the rest of the day. 'Your friend's a laugh, isn't he? The things he comes out with.'

'Is George upset at not being allowed to conjure here?' Kit asked.

'Somewhat. Do you think he's ready to perform in public?'

'Not in front of an adult public. Although the Aldhouse birthday party will have given him confidence, I'm sure.'

Hathaway, who did not seem put out by her host's departure nor to have taken offence at the statement of his purpose for making himself scarce, had been listening intently to what Kit and I were saying, her eyes focussing on the fair-headed handsome man beside me in a way I could not exactly interpret. She was certainly not appraising Kit for his looks nor it seemed had she altogether written him off, regardless of his composure, as a person in need of her psychiatric offices. Her eyes narrowed then and one of her thin smiles stretched across the discreetly painted lips, a smile not directed at Kit but towards herself, a small smile of triumph as if, without the need to interrogate this guest, she had located a chink in his armour which, with one of the arrows in her quiver, she would pierce when the time was ripe. It was possible they'd met before somewhere and she was trying to recall the circumstances or waiting until Kit recognized her from the past. She prompted him.

'I didn't catch your name.'

'Christopher.'

'No, your surname. I am Roz Hathaway.'

'How do you do,' Kit said. He turned to me. 'Shall we make tracks? Go back to my place, have a cup of tea, and relax?'

'Are your duties over here?'

'According to the book on wedding etiquette I bought for the occasion, yes, they are. Did you know one of the best man's jobs is to play a prank on the groom.'

'Not on his wedding day, surely?'

'At his stag do.'

Neither of us said goodbye to Professor Hathaway who we left flanked with empty seats on her either side.

CHAPTER X

It was the first time Kit and I had had a good talk. We'd sometimes
exchanged a few words when I dropped George off or collected him
after his magic lessons but as often as not he would bicycle there and
back, bringing occasional news such as Kit's incipient engagement,
'He says I'll still be able to come for lessons after he's married,' or his
prowess in the armed services. He had been in the S.A.S. 'He was,'
George reported, 'one of their prime assassins. Of course, he is sworn
not to say much more than that.'

'Of course.'

'Now he is a medaller.'

'With whom does he meddle?'

'That's not funny, dad.'

'It's funny a bit.'

'It's not funny lots. I mean he makes medals.'

'For a living.'

'I suppose.'

I asked Kit if it were a profitable calling.

'Keeps the wolf from the door, not much more than that. I'd do
better if I could take on government or military work but when I left
The Regiment I was told I wouldn't be allowed to tout for official
business for some reason best known to the powers that be. I do resto-
rations and repairs, civil decorations only. My main source of income
is in the sports market, casting gongs for golf club presidents to hang
round each others' necks. A bit of freemasonic regalia comes my way
and occasionally a cranky secret society wants something done. I'm
working now on one for a local chap who's a big noise in some cult or
other. "There is no religion higher than Truth": that's what I have to
incise on the obverse of the thing. I suppose it's an arguable maxim.
It has to be enclosed within a hexagram which is the devil to engrave,
believe you me.'

Then we began to talk about magic. I mentioned my concern that
George's enthusiasm for conjuring could lead him into the realms of
the supernatural in which for a while I had unhealthily dabbled. Kit
thought not.

'George is a strictly practical fellow. I am sure he will not stray off the
straight and narrow. Like all boys he wants to run before he can walk.

Big stuff, that's what he's keen to do, stage illusions. Levitations, escapes, sword cabinets, vanishing elephants, anything with flashy apparatus. Boys love apparatus. And of course his hands are still a bit too small to accomplish a lot of the sleight-of-hand needed for playing-card and coin work. By the way, I was very impressed by George's double-lift. You must have taught him that. And the little finesse at the end. Is that your doing as well?'

Kit was referring to the sleight where the magician appears to take one card from the top of a pack but secretly takes the top two cards.

'That's quite old. I learned it as a boy. It is called the Braue replacement.'

'Sounds like the title of a spy novel. Would that the same Braue who co-wrote *The Royal Road to Card Magic*?'

'Yes. I think I got it from there.'

'And the little finger break to start it all off. Who's idea was that?'

'It's an American control, I think. They call it the pinky count.'

'They would. Americans are such poufs.'

Kit occupied the ground floor of a cottage at the river end of the village. We entered through a gate let into the wall of a small garden in which Kit had built his medallist's workshop. French windows led into the sitting-room, from there into a glass verandah running to the street door at the opposite end of the house. His interest was at once made apparent by a framed print of Bosch's, or was it Brueghel's, 'Conjuror?' Aldhouse would know. Among the spectators gathered in front of the magician's table was a tall, fair-haired woman, a cut, a considerable cut, above the proletarian sprinkling of onlookers. I remarked on her resemblance to the new Lady Wendon. Kit showed no interest in that comparison.

'I never bothered with the cups and balls,' he said, referring to the effect with which the mountebank was deceiving his village audience with the exception of a bespectacled pickpocket who was engaged on a deception of his own. 'Come into the kitchen. Shall we have tea or would you prefer to go on with wine? I'm no kind of a drinker myself but I think there's a bottle or two round here somewhere. Not champagne, I'm afraid. Did you ever think of becoming a professional magician?'

'For a while when I was about George's age. Then I messed about with spiritualism until I was warned off that and returned, newborn, to the three-quarter line-out and the slip cordon. What about you?'

'I gave it up because I was such a bad liar. I never felt easy about having to lie to my audience. Lying is part of a magician's stock-in-trade. For better or worse, he has to lie all the time. Pick a card, any card, you have complete freedom of choice (no you don't), nothing up my sleeve (yes, there is), *equivoque*. The hypocrisy of it all turned me off eventually.'

'And now George has returned you to a life of deceit.'

Spoken in fun, my remark generated across Kit's face a momentary spasm of concern, not far off alarm, as if he had been found out in some opaque business not at all related to the magic arts, indeed to any form of frivolity, with which he hoped he might never be confronted. Could he be using an inferior metal in the casting of his medals, fiddling his tax bills, or, in the way that Backstairs Bailey was rumoured never to have flown an aeroplane, lying about his service in the elite regiment of the S.A.S? For a short moment, the second or two of this disconcertion from which he quickly composed himself, it seemed as if Kit had aged at least ten years. Was he in fact rather older than he represented himself to others, a man approaching forty rather than one in his early thirties, if as much? I had him down as being about twenty-eight. George might have told me that. Now it crossed my mind that some daily artifice might be required in order to maintain this apparent youthfulness or an operation undergone to tighten facial skin now in his forties beginning to sag. All the same, I had never perceived anything about the way he held himself and his manner of speech to suggest vanity, nor here and now, as he regained his composure, could I detect any contrivance in the smoothness of the skin, the evenness of the teeth, the curl and colour of the blond hair.

To put things back on track. I mentioned to Kit the Academy's SWOT plan to present to our students a forgotten figure in our various lines of country. I asked who his forgotten conjuror would be.

'Dr Jaks. Unquestionably. He was Swiss, I believe, or German. He had a wonderfully constructed hollow box labelled 'The Book of Mystery' that held his entire act. He was a uniquely close-up artist. For a stage performer, let me think: Kalanag? No, horrible man, nazi probably. Talking of magicians from the olden days, did George tell you about the eighteenth-century Bottle Conjuror?'

'No.'

'Then he's a very naughty boy. I asked him to specifically because there is a reference to the originator of the act's living in these parts that I thought you might like to include in the local history book George says you're writing. Hang on, I'll get the reference.'

I swivelled round on my kitchen stool and examined some of the prints on the wall behind me. I was faced with a generously proportioned, altogether unfamiliar, chromo-lithograph looking as if it had been unfolded from a Victorian magazine and put into a frame. Within the marbled walls of an oriental palace, a boy about George's age faced an assembly of a very different constitution from the one gathered to watch Bosch's itinerant juggler. A huge snake, a python or a boa-constrictor, had been charmed out of its straw basket by the pipings of a bearded fakir seated cross-legged on the stone floor and into the arms of this boy who, at full stretch, held the hypnotized creature triumphantly above his head. In contrast to Bosch's entertainment where the spectators were mainly women, the two Indians were watched uniquely by men. Nine men and a boy much the age of the snake handler made up the small attendance.

The painter had placed his easel diagonally behind the two performers, bidding us observe the spectators as well as the protagonists whom even from this chosen angle he had managed to portray as no more than travelling mountebanks at the beck and call of the men for whom they performed. He had presented the central figure of this audience, sprawled in an armchair and opulently clothed, as the one in authority over a shabby entourage for whom no seating had been provided. There could be no doubt that it was he who had given the order for this private exhibition of wonder-working, at the same time demanding somewhere comfortable to sit while the performance was in progress. This commander's auxiliaries, muffled each one in differently patterned, probably tribal, robes, squatted on the floor or propped themselves against the blue-tiled wall that formed a background to a scene proposing an eventuality of a fatal nature.

There were suggestions that the taming of the enormous serpent, admirable though that ought to have been, taking into consideration the infirmity of one of the jugglers and the youth of the other, had not been well received. An atmosphere of considerable menace perpended within this marble palace, exuding primarily from the seated emir. He looked barbarous to a degree: short-tempered: not to be trifled with. Any lowering of standards might result in his barking an order for the performers, man and boy, to be run through with the long spears on which for the moment his posse reposefully leant. One could not quite understand why the boy had no clothes on. Nakedness may have been employed by the artist to emphasize the potentate's finery, the territorial raiments of his entourage, and the lowliness of the two street performers who had been ordered, on pain of death, to put on this entertainment.

Kit came back. 'Now then, this Bottle Conjuror. Here's the piece about him in an old *Genii* I used to subscribe to. Take it home with you.'

I asked whether the boy in the picture was the one who charmed the snake or the cross-legged ascetic by the side of the basket whose fluted notes could have aroused the python to coil around his assistant's neck.

'Probably the old fellow is doing the charming, the boy a mere assistant. Later in the show he may be thrown into the basket and have a few knives stuck through him.'

'The Indian version of sawing a woman in half?'

'Exactly.'

We began to talk about old theatre posters announcing magical performers and performances. George and I had found a website advertising reproductions onto T-shirts of these vintage placards from what could be called the golden age of stage magic. Westerners in tail-coats or satin knee breeches, pig-tailed Chinamen in national costume, stared out at the passer-by with hypnotic eyes or were portrayed going through their stage acts, while little red familiars with forked tails, summoned by the magicians to assist them with their magic, in the way Amos was hoping to recruit King Solomon's demons in furtherance of his ambitions, cackled in the corners of these lurid illustrations. George had fallen for one particular poster designed for the escape artist, Houdini, 'Houdini in the Water Torture Cell.' The performer, wearing a one-piece bathing-suit and manacled hand and foot, had been hoisted upside-down by a crane and lowered into a large tank filled to the brim with water. He could be seen through the glass of his prison calmly contemplating his fate. I asked Kit if he knew it.

'Indeed I do. It's one of the best posters ever. It says underneath, "Failure means a drowning death".'

'That's the caption on the shirt.'

I was becoming garrulous. I always let things run away with me when talking about George. Fathers are often lyrically expansive about their daughters, sketching in for the listener a full picture of the intelligence, the high spirits, the cuteness or, dependent on their age, the beauty of their girl children and their contribution to a sunny family life. About their sons they have little to add to the proposition that they are, by and large, a pain in the arse. I recalled Cyrus's father's disparaging reference to him as the *sprog*. 'Nice of you to have had the sprog,' he had said and had then tried to reimburse me financially for the inconvenience of looking after this spawned impediment to a life of ease. George's take-over of my life, that is to say the sudden revelation that he was the only person in the world I truly loved or would ever love, an event to be compared to a spiritual conversion which certainly loosens the tongue of the sanctified man who never tires of describing his rapture and is anxious as well to lead others into the fold, serves to explain a talkativeness disposed, if not forcibly silenced, to get out of control. I spoke some words of apology.

Kit waved aside any such intemperance.

'No, no, go on. I like hearing about George's and your lives together. Did you buy him the shirt? He has a good broad chest that would show off a picture like that to advantage.'

'We were just about to buy it when George saw another poster he liked better. Unfortunately. Have you ever heard of the magician, Harold?'

'Never. What an odd name for a conjuror.'

'He was a Frenchman. The name sounds more impressive in French. 'Arold, also known as the Executioner, *le coupeur de têtes*. Monsieur Harold is wearing striped knee-breeches like the Papal Guard's and has just lopped off a girl's head which he's lifting up by her hair. Blood pours down from the severed neck. On stage with him are three hooded assistants in red robes looking like torturers from the Inquisition. One of them is holding a dinner plate ready to receive the severed head. George badgered me to buy the shirt for him. I thought it too bloodthirsty so I said no: at first.'

'But he won you over?'

'Yes.'

Rules about the designs on shirts had been laid down some years earlier and it was agreed they should proclaim an allegiance to a team, a band, or a hobby, as opposed to announcing personal traits, good or bad, or advice to others – 'Just do it' for instance – which were not permitted. Maniacs running amok with axes, a common theme in our local souvenir shops, were also under the ban. Harold had narrowly avoided falling into that category.

'The shirt arrived yesterday. George is going to wear it for you to admire the next time he comes over.'

'I look forward to seeing it.'

I asked why it was always women who were the magician's victims, locked into cabinets for swords to be run through them, got themselves sawn in half.

'All they're good for.'

Kit spoke bitterly. Perhaps, in the past, there had been an unhappy love affair. He corrected himself almost at once. 'Except my fiancée of course. I call myself a lucky man.' He indicated a colour photograph in a silver frame. A young woman stretched herself out across a seaside wall. She wore a striped cotton dress. A split skirt revealed suntanned legs. At her back, a rust-stained protuberance, most likely a capstan, rearing upwards against the background of the azure waters, violently challenged the immaculateness of the dress and, for the matter of that, the modesty of the posing mannequin.

It was hard to disagree about the girl's allure, if that was what Kit meant when he referred to his good fortune. There was, however, one serious obstacle to her becoming being Kit's wife. The woman was dead.

Here was Melissa, the young model, killed in an air-crash, I'd heard, who had been my girl friend, Sylvia's, and my companion at the spa hotel, an episode memorable for the discovery that my bank account had been mysteriously credited with fifty thousand pounds, the event that had radically changed my life. What in heaven's name could have possessed Kit, a handsome enough fellow whom many women would find attractive, to frame a glossy print from a fashion shoot of some twenty years ago – almost before he was born now I came to think of it – and pass it off as a photograph of his fiancée? One could understand a man like Ganson doing that sort of thing, advertising to his friends that there was a beautiful woman in his life when in reality none such existed, but surely Kit had no such reason to resort to this sort of aggrandisement.

These conceptions lasted only for a moment. Of course I had the wrong person. Kit's fiancée looked like Melissa. She was Melissa's double, one could go so far. Most likely, the fashion house where

131

Melissa had worked still turned out the identically patterned beach-wear of Kit's girlfriend and had posed her in the same location they had used for Melissa all those years ago because of her resemblance to the model they had employed when they'd first put that particular garment on the market. I said some words agreeing with Kit's estimate of his fiancée's good looks, then we plunged back into our talk of the theory and practice of conjuring until it was time for me to go and pick up George from school. Kit was far more knowledgeable than I about magic, so much so that I suggested to Ganson the next day that he might be taken on the staff to teach the history of the art. This went down well. He rated the idea highly, treating it almost as if it had been one of his shots in the arm.

'I don't see why not,' he said. 'Exeter University has a department of esoteric studies. There is something of the sort at one of the Swedish universities, Gothenburg, I seem to remember. If I did employ him, he'd better come as a visiting lecturer. Scottie McLeod may think your friend's muscling in on his theological syllabus if we give him a separate department. By the way, I hope you didn't mention our schoolboy pranks with the planchette or whatever it was we used.'

'I didn't mean real magic, I meant conjuring.'

'Oh, I see.'

Ganson was doubtful about that, fearing perhaps that a faculty given up to a branch of popular entertainment might get swallowed up by the dancing school next door.

'We'll have Madam Tumbleova recruiting him for her own ends,' he said.

Nevertheless, an arrangement was made for Kit to conduct two seminars on the history of legerdemain. A practical demonstration made up part of these talks where Ganson had been in attendance.

'Mr Buller knocked us all for six,' he said. 'George is a lucky boy to have him as a mentor. Especially at no cost. By the way, Stairs says we may have to shave a groat or two off Mr Buller's fee.'

A few days after the wedding two unrelated incidents occurred, only later fusing, like a terrible and secret weapon of war when two apparently harmless chemicals dropped from the sky interact into a poisonous amalgam, choking the lungs, blistering the skin, stopping short of death in order to allow for the adversary's glee at seeing his enemies incapacitated and in pain.

There had been a tense atmosphere at breakfast time. George was due to have an audition to join the school choir. Afterwards he would go straight on to Kit's to show off his Harold T-shirt. He looked up from his plate.

'Dad, I've got a nosebleed.'

'Lie back in your chair, then, tilt your head back. And I'll plug up your nose.'

I found a tissue and wiped the blob of tomato sauce from George's right nostril.

'That's not funny.'

'It's funny a bit.'

'It's not funny lots.'

'I've got a question for you. You know pigeons?'

'Yes, I know pigeons. And don't ask me if they do It because yes they do. They lay eggs and sit on them. Now, stop trying to wriggle out of the voice test.'

'I know pigeons lay eggs. Everybody knows that. What I'm asking is why do they always stop in mid-coo. They go "coo, coo, coo, coo, cc...", stop. Maybe another make of bird, a bigger one's, told them to shut up.'

'I think that's probably a question Auntie Salt could have answered.'

George stood up. 'Dad, I'm really nervous. I think my bowels will turn to water.'

'Like Sills's?'

'No, he was sick in a bucket. I might be that too. I'd better get going. See you about six.'

'Going you are not. Going you are nowhere near being. You are a mess, you are an urchin in rags and tatters, a disgrace to yourself, to your school, to your father. First of all, Harold needs hiding with a shirt until you get to Kit's: a clean shirt what's more. I will not insist upon a tie, merely pass the concept across your eyes. And you must wear your blazer and your grey trousers, rather than the ones you've not quite got on. And a pair, note the word, pair, of socks. And sensible shoes. Laced up.'

George occasionally mistook, or feigned to mistake, a serious command for innocuous banter. 'You are messing about, aren't you?'

'I am in deadly earnest.'

'You don't look in deadly earnest. You just look deadly. Daddy looks deadly. Deadly daddy. Deadly diddly daddy. Daddly deadly doddly badly.' George flung his arms from side to side in a fashionably jerky measure accompanied by a string of words he formed into a rap song denigrating parenthood in several of its branches. A foul pair of trainers was kicked off and sent scudding across the kitchen floor as the dance grew ever more frenzied. These were delaying tactics of course, time strung out until it would become too late for George to attend his audition.

'You have three minutes to find some decent clothes to wear today otherwise I shall go to your room and find them for you.'

These were words heavy with menace. Entry to the loft that George had made his own was forbidden without written permission. A calligraphically inscribed pass giving exact times of arrival and departure was occasionally issued which permitted me to climb the ladder on the stairs and push open the trapdoor labelled with George's name and the initials K.B.E.

'Knight of the British Empire?'

'Knock Before Entering.'

George got off without his tie, otherwise looking presentable enough. I settled to my village history and then remembered the magazine Kit had lent me that contained the article he thought might be relevant to my research. It reproduced an anecdote extracted from the diary of an eighteenth-century historian concerning a theatrical production of an unusual kind:

'My Lord M———, who, at the time of which I write, the Year of Our Lord 1749, resided at D———— where he had acquired a Manor, and in that village and throughout the Kingdom, much to the distress of his Step-Mother, the Duchess of ——————, was given to the sort of Frolicks the better performed by a Stripling of fifteen years of age than a Gentleman of four-and-forty, one time propelling a French Savant by name

Montesquieu into a Tub of Cold Water. Another Jape was essayed which for once failed in its amusement. In the Year of wh. I speak, he did cause to be announced on the playbills that at the Haymarket Theatre London there would be presented a remarkable phenomenon, *viz.* a man who would upon an ordinary Walking Cane sound the notes of any known instrument whether stringed or blown upon and wd thereafter before the eyes of the Town shrink himself to so small a size as to be laden into a Quart Bottle. There within its depths he would sing out a selection of Glees and englazed yet within its walls venture correctly to identify any of the Noblemen occupying the Boxes who cared to mask themselves and present themselves thus disguised before the Conjuror as he was inclosed in his Vessel. *Alicujus rei summum habuisse facultatem*, as old Pliny bids, our mysterious Merlin proposed that, as a finale, he would communicate with the Souls of Dead Men & speak a Message of comfort to any of the Company desirous of meeting once more an acquaintance who had passed beyond the Tomb and that Message would be in the very Tongue to be instantly recognized as that of the personage who had gone before.

For this Enterprize wh. I need not say came to naught and for which the disapprobation of the Town resulted in the demolition of the Playhouse, My Lord M—— was aided by a Milord S— G— also known as Racozky, a Count of Hungarian extraction for whom His Lordship had caused to be built in his Manor of D—— a most secluded dwelling so well hid that no prying eye cd discern its where-abouts. Now this Count who had the Ear of the King and who could manufacture the finest Diamonds and those not to be distinguished from the real stones found in the earth was reputed as well to have discovered the Elixir of Life & to have been born full One Hundred and Thirty Years since, for all he looked a quarter part of those past days. Wherefore he was so urgently sought out by so many people wishing to be taught his Skills and to be apprised of his Secret of eternal Youth that when he lived under the Ægis of Lord M——, he went under the name of Mr. Welldone.

Ciel, as Ganson might say. Here was a discovery indeed. It might not add much to my village history but it added a great deal towards the identity of our mysterious neighbour. The Marquisate of M—— referred to by the diarist was long defunct. I already had a note that the second Marquess was responsible for building our church and for endowing the village in perpetuity with several acres of common land on a section of which our cricket club functioned. What was new to me was the existence of the mysterious S--- G--- 'also known as Racozky,' alias Mr Welldone.'

The current Mr Welldone, our saviour from the car crash, must be a scion of this noble house, maintaining the bourgeois pseudonym from centuries before for reasons best known to himself, playfully perhaps, for there seemed to be something of the larrikin as well as of the aristocrat in his general deportment that had made his ancestor a willing accomplice in the Marquess's theatrical jape. His central European nationality went some way to explaining the Mozartian likeness that had struck me when we first met. Probably, he occupied his ancestor's house, the 'most secluded dwelling' referred to by the diarist, the location of which was still evading discovery. Our excursion within the grounds of a royal park suggested that the latest in the line of 'Welldones' still 'had the ear' of the monarch. His habitation might well lie within that domain where his car had been put through its paces with George and me on board.

About four o'clock, the doorbell rang. I took it to be George home from Kit's earlier than expected. I buzzed him in and got on with the book. There was a commotion on the stairs. Male voices were raised in dispute. A comic scene was revealed. Two men built in the mould of Drake and, to judge from what they had to say, sharing his chronic dislike of physical labour, were toiling upwards with a gargantuan washing-machine. Chrome and enamel glinting in the dim light of the stairway betokened the same costliness and efficient mechanism as Mr Welldone's Flying Spur. This was Roz Hathaway's doing. 'Is it really true you haven't got a washing machine? We must see if we can't address the issue.' Those were her words to me after the incident at the wedding when Ganson had poured wine over himself. Here then was her bribe or a bribe offered by Oo May fashions at her instigation. Now we have presented you with this enviable and valuable household appliance, the message ran, you will naturally wish to revoke the letter your son wrote requesting a fee for parading our name across his clothing.

The machine must go back where it came from. That was my first thought, although to ask the men to reverse their upwards journey could risk sending them and the machine cascading backwards down the staircase, or at best unleash a mutinous volley of oaths for the double inconvenience undergone. Bribe or no bribe, it had to be said that the machine would prove a godsend. George, who would never carry anything at all if he could get away with it – 'I might have to protect you from muggers' was his excuse for always walking along empty-handed – would be absolved from the embarrassment of trundling down our washing to the launderette and back again, a journey he was afraid might be overseen by his school friends. In the event of our keeping the machine, there would, of course, be no question of caving in to the Professor's demand to withdraw the Oo May letter in exchange for its donation.

By now, it stood on the landing. The men mopped their brows.

'Cup of tea would go down, mate. Before we have to turn off the water, like. And the lekky. If you could point us to the meter...'

I couldn't, but George would know. I rang Kit and asked him to tell George to come back as quickly as he could. He arrived almost instantaneously. He was hot, out of breath, unusually confused.

'You were quick.'

'Kit drove me back. Is everything all right, dad? We thought you'd had an accident or were ill or something.'

I explained the situation, mentioning that, if George was of the same mind, I would accept Oo May's gift. I made it clear at the same time that we would not be deterred from our battle for some sort of remuneration for advertising their goods. 'My guess is they'll offer you five pounds a month for a year in the hope that you ...'

'Will f. off?'

'...will get off their backs, was the way I was going to put it.'

'Cool,' George said. 'I'll save all the money up and then ... what's fifty-two times eight?'

'What's fifty times eight?'

'That's not what I asked.'

'Tell me.'

'Four hundred.'

'What's two times eight?'

'Sixteen.'

'What's four hundred plus sixteen?'

'Four hundred and sixteen. I get it. So the eight pounds a week we save by not going to the launderette plus Oo May's, what's twelve fives, oh sixty, can go towards the wrist-chopper which I really need for my stage act.'

I sat at the kitchen table while George selected a place for the machine, guided the electricians around the intricate wiring, lugged things about. The general upheaval was succeeded by a great calm. The men had drunk their tea: installed the apparatus: accepted a tip: gone their way. The machine shone invitingly. George and I agreed it would be fun to put it to the test there and then.

He poured some washing powder into the entrails of the machine. 'What shall we load it up with?'

'Sheets, pillowcases.'

'No, 'cos, basically, if we strip our beds we'd have to remake them. And that would interrupt supper time which it nearly is.'

'You're right. Bad idea. Forget it.'

'What day's today?'

'Wednesday.'

'Then tomorrow's clean clothes day. Let's throw in everything we usually take to the laundry.'

'Everything we're wearing now, you mean? And the dirty things in the bathroom?'

'Those too.' George was already unbuttoning his shirt.

'And present ourselves naked before the all-seeing eye of the God of Cleanliness and Pure Living?'

'Don't be poetic, father.' George took off his shoes, the sensible shoes I had instructed him to wear that morning.

'I'm going to put my socks in. Definitely. You should put yours in too. They'll be as smelly as mine, smellier probably. There is a often a distinct smell of socks in this kitchen. That is a fact known to all. What are you staring at, dad?'

George, with his white school shirt dangling from his hand, stood before me bare-chested.

'Where's Harold?'

'Harold?'

'The T-shirt.'

George made no reply as if my remarking on the absence – or presence – of anything he was wearing was an observation of such gratuitous absurdity that it could be reasonably ignored. 'You had it on when you went out. You wore it specially to show Kit.'

'Did I? I've forgotten.'

'How can you have forgotten? It was the whole point of your going to see him. Was it so baking hot at Kit's place that you needed to strip yourself to the waist?'

George shrugged his shoulders.

'Well?'

'I spilt something on it. Juice. Orange juice. So I took it off, basically. I'd have brought it home only you ringing up in such a panic made me forget it. Pity. It could have been washed with the rest of our stuff. Come on, dad, trousers next, there's no need to be shy. And we'll need a few more bits to fill this thing up to its full capacity.' George whirled around the kitchen grabbing at a towel, dish-cloths, an apron, anything he could find that could be piled into the machine. 'And this and this. Now, stand back, dad. I'm going to switch on.'

We watched, entranced, near-naked, as the machine began its work. Our transfixion was not complete, however. George kept looking at me oddly but when our eyes met he turned away and focused again on our new totem and its Cyclopean eye that swivelled and watered and filled with mucus and cleared and wept again for the votaries who stood before it and for what would be their fate. Then the telephone rang.

George ran to answer it.

CHAPTER XII

'I nivver tooched it,' McLeod said. He unstrapped his pads with a tearing sound as if he were rending his own flesh. He launched them through the air, one after the other, in the direction of the scorer, identifiable as Hawley Fawcett, the parish verger to whom Ganson had behaved so rudely at the wedding breakfast. Fawcett ducked the missiles and carefully entered McLeod's dismissal in his analysis. The next batsman trudged in. The victim of a bad decision as he saw it settled on the grass next to me and lit a cigarette.

'Rotten umpire. Canna see: that's his trouble. The man is stone blind behind those specs of his. Who's the wee bairn bowling donkey drops? Is he in our side?'

George, practising in the nets on the boundary edge, would not have been amused to hear his leg breaks spoken of with such derision.

'My son. He'll win the match for us singlehanded.'

'Good luck to him,' McLeod said. 'If Jack keeps upholding rotten appeals when the other lot goes in, you're very probably right'. The game progressed. Another wicket fell.

'There goes another one, thanks to four-eyes,' McLeod said. 'Got it wrong again, shouldn't wonder. By the way, I've got a book-title to add to our always-to-be-found-in-bookshops list: *Six Dramas of Calderón.*'

'"Freely Translated by Edward Fitzgerald." That's a good one. There was a copy in that big London place. What prompted Fitzgerald to translate Calderón?'

George came over and asked me to bowl to him.

'I really hope I don't have to bat.'

'You'll be fine. You enjoy batting.'

In due course, George's eleven took the field. The opposition's opening pair proved resilient. George was put on to bowl. Just then, there came a brief hold-up in proceedings. Someone, a woman, a tall woman, was marching purposefully, if not especially quickly, across the field of play, initiating the stoppage. Some of the fielders sat down. George folded his arms resignedly. I recognized Professor Hathaway. Stiletto heels on the yielding surface of the grass hampered any brisker progression aimed at by this intruder whose ignorance of the game of cricket led her to assume it was played only on the pitch which she carefully avoided as she passed among athletes she took to be on their break.

She made for me. A high heel pierced the turf close to my fingers. I wondered how easy it would be to snap it off, or whether, with a bit of luck, it might imbed itself so deeply in the earth as to trip her up and send her flat on her face. She leant over me and put her hands on her knees as if she were talking to a stretchered invalid.

'I'd be glad of a moment of your time.'

'If it's about the letter, we are sticking to our guns. Washing machine or no washing machine. For which many thanks, by the way.'

'Oh, the famous letter,' she said as if she had forgotten all about it. She gave one of her caring smiles and closed her eyes for a moment as if she were experiencing a stab of pain. 'I wish it were about the letter. What I have to say does concern your son, though. I see he's out there now. He won't come over, will he? This must be strictly between ourselves. No, he seems to be involved with the game.'

I wondered how it came about that she knew what George looked like. He had not been at home the morning she had called.

'Go on.'

'I have some troubling news. Shall we sit on that bench? The ground seems a tad damp. Now, what I am obliged to report will come as a painful experience to you, I am afraid. Your child is the victim of abuse by an adult male. For the present, I am naming no names but you will know who I am talking about when I say the abuser and I met briefly at the wedding party the other week. I have taken no action personally, thus far, although morally and legally I am bound to do so. That should be your duty too, as a parent.'

'I assume this is yet another ploy to make me withdraw my son's letter. A disgusting one, furthermore.'

'It is nothing of the kind. The man of whom I speak has been in prison and in my opinion should be in prison again. I'm telling you what I have seen with my own eyes. It was quite by chance that I came upon the two of them in a compromising situation. The child was on this man's knee. Clothing was disarranged.'

'Yours?'

'You seem to be taking this very casually, if you don't mind me saying. Surely you can't fail to appreciate the seriousness of an issue such as this or am I to suppose the unthinkable, that you condone Mr Buller's inappropriate relations with your underage son? There, now I have given the man a name.'

'And where was this inappropriateness supposed to be going on?'

'In the man's home. I happened to be passing his house when I caught sight of them through the window.'

'You couldn't have caught sight of them through any window on the street side of the house because there are none. You must, therefore, have been in the garden at the back. Broken in, not to put too fine a point on it.'

'That's as may be. But aren't you thankful I did so? What concerns me, and what concerns all decent people, is the action you are going to take. You will act, will you not?'

'I will act immediately. By putting an end to this conversation.'

Here was the cue for the ever-ready indulgent smile. This time it was overlaid with an oblique slyness, the therapist's caring mask overridden by the insolence of the extortionist. The eyes narrowed and slid downwards. She smiled in triumph at her lethal shoes.

'I'll say no more just now. You are in denial of course. That is only natural.' She laid a hand on my shoulder. I shook it off, stood up, and walked away.

Well, then. Things were hotting up. The Professor was no longer in the business of bribery. This was blackmail. The unscrupulousness of big business and the lengths to which it was prepared to stretch the boundaries of ethics to ensure its continuing profitability were exemplified in the conditions Hathaway had placed before me. Promise us you and your son will not take your little joke any further or we will accuse an innocent man of a vicious crime. All you need to do is to 'cease and desist' from making the demands on our clothing company and the threat will be withdrawn. It was a fiendish and a disgusting ploy: implying my son's traumatic disturbance: accusing me of being party to its cause: implicating Kit whom the Professor had met only at the wedding where she would have got wind of his tutoring George in the magic arts: an ultimatum that, if it were disobeyed, could impair, indeed potentially destroy, the lives of a father, his son, and a family friend: all in the course of her trade commitments. I gave thought to whether the scheme had been hatched over Oo May's boardroom table or whether it was Hathaway's own invention for which, if she proved successful in the withdrawal of George's requests, she would earn herself some sort of commission on top of whatever the firm paid for her pastoral guidances.

Never before had I experienced anger on the scale that now over-whelmed me. I lived, of course, among angry people, Ganson, my father-in-law, Scottie McLeod, all of whom could ignite in me passion enough to join them in railing against our fellow men and women, only to calm down as they themselves would calm down after a few minutes when we would then laugh away our intolerant outbursts. This new anger was an anger of a volcanic nature sufficient, had Hathaway still been by my side, for me to have felled her with a single blow of McLeod's cricket bat and trampled her underfoot until she screamed for mercy.

There were those who would argue I had little cause for complaint. The prank George and I had played had turned sour. The best plan now would be to capitulate. That would be the end of it. Would it not? Then, by her words of how, in support of her lies, Hathaway had said she had observed George on Kit's knee, I was reminded of the day her washing machine had been delivered and my bewilderment that George was no longer wearing the 'Harold' top he had put on when he left the house in the morning and his embarrassment when I asked him why he had taken it off. Was that the day she had found him in Kit's arms, stripped by him of that T-shirt, 'his clothing disarranged' in her prissy phrase. I had a terrible suspicion that this might be the case. It could explain why George had been so confused when questioned about 'Harold,' a reaction I had then taken for incomprehension at my concern for a mislaid item of clothing, an event of almost daily occurrence in our domestic routine. Except, of course, it was an item in which he took great pride, a garment to be flaunted rather than casually discarded just because, so he said, he had spilt something down it. Now I came to think of it, the suspicion had briefly crossed my mind at the time that something was afoot, something to have a pernicious outcome.

In this case though, I told myself that such a thing was out of the question. The idea could be dismissed as absurd since it was absurd to see George as an object of desire, absurd too for him to look on Kit in the same light. Except, of course, Kit was a good-looking fellow in his way and so was the boy he might have seduced, lying lulled in Kit's arms as he listened to the stories of his glory days in the SAS, probably as chimerical a career as Bailey's flying exploits, put about to impress everyone that he was a true-hearted servant of the nation instead of a re-offending jail-bird of the seediest kind. The tornado of my rage arose from Hathaway and swept upon Kit. Kit was guilty, guilty beyond any doubt whatever.

I would have to act as the Professor had said I must, there were no two ways about that, but what sort of action should I take? Beat Kit to a pulp? March him down to the police station where he'd be sent for trial at which George would have to give evidence behind a screen, evidence wrung from him by heavily breathing policewomen who had muddled him with dirty questions? Consign my son to a psychiatrist, a priest, or a counsellor, likely to be every bit as obnoxious as Professor Hathaway? Which of the two, her or Kit, I had to ask myself, was the more destructive of my son's wellbeing and – more selfishly if I faced facts – of my own. I looked at George as he was consulted by his captain about where he wanted his fielders. The captain nodded, gave his orders, tousled George's hair. Was he too...?

As well as not knowing how to handle Kit, I had no idea of how to ask George if the accusation were true which I was now certain that it was. Things began to fall into line. George had said he had never met Kit's fiancée although her framed photograph owned a prominent place in the living-room. There was no fiancée. The picture – or, as I had once suspected, a picture of a model cut from a magazine – was put on show as a blind. Other, very different, pictures in the house reflected Kit's real obsession, the coloured print above the kitchen stove, for instance, of a pert cabin-boy calling from his galley, 'Try My Soup.' A second composition, the reproduction of Jean-Léon Gérôme's 'Snake Charmer,' I had taken as a reflection of Kit's interest in stage magic. Now, it offered a very different interpretation. The taming of the python by the two fakirs may, for a time, have amused – and mystified – the picture's chieftain and his motley crew. Then, as the boy lifts the great snake in triumph above his head, he reveals to his audience his full nakedness. A second elongation, disproportionate enough when compared with the first to have raised a smile or two among the onlookers, has been put on view. That was what the chieftain had come to see.

It was not to my credit, or so it would appear to the Professor and her kind, that I was less concerned about George's wellbeing than I was about the fear that Kit might surmount, might have already surmounted, my place in George's heart. George had said, on the day we had rid ourselves of Yseult Pash, 'Let's not ever have anyone else coming between us.' There had been occasions recently when George had seemed less ready than in the past to initiate a conversation in the way he used to by saying, 'Dad, I've got a question for you,' more aloof too or perhaps I meant more independent, less reliant upon me for guidance or as a source of information. Here were signs that could be interpreted as a dwindling of affection. I could of course ask him if he loved me as much as ever he had, but the interrogative, 'Do you love me?' by whomever it is put, wives, husbands, sons, daughters, girl-friends, boy-friends, is susceptible of only an affirmative answer: whether that answer be true or false.

George would have to be interrogated before anything at all could be done. I thought long and hard about how to broach the subject, how I could tactfully put the question that, spoken from the shoulder, would be 'Are you sleeping with Kit?' and at the same time absolve him from being an accomplice in a criminal act. Naturally, no mention could be made that that was what it constituted. How was the interview – itself an absurd word – to be conducted? In confrontational mood, 'It has come to my notice,' or a paternal one when I saw myself puffing at a pipe I had never smoked and offering pastoral advice I knew to be contrived? Each role produced clichés: each approach smacked of melodrama. I did not want to fight with George, spoil his day, as Molly would have put it. Yet, a melodramatic approach might well be the only way to get at the truth.

The thing was that I already knew the answers to the questions I would have to put. George by nature was a happy boy, happy and un-worried. Of that I was certain. I knew him well enough by now to have been alerted to any anxiety he was undergoing however deeply it lay buried, although in fact it is the traumas that are deepest-lying that, un-known to himself, the sufferer puts on show rather than the superficial nervousnesses, a fear of spiders, shall we say? that he has no trouble in concealing. And so, following on from that, it had to be supposed that George, who never missed an opportunity for bicycling round to Kit if occasion offered, couldn't care less about what was going on.

My mind, eased by the conclusion that no harm had come to George, roved further afield, into wilder landscapes. I wondered, for instance, whether George and Cyrus had played about when they were in my big double-bed together. I recalled Cyrus's enigmatic words when he had posed himself decoratively, sword in hand, on the staircase wearing his knee-length tunic beneath which, he gave out, he was naked. He had hinted at the impropriety, or he could have meant the temptation, offered by this condition. 'It might be dangerous,' he had said. Molly may have perceived a sensuality in Cyrus when she had spoken of him as 'big for his age.' If Cyrus had met Kit (and I could not remember if he had) had he recognized him as a lover of boys, granted him the same 'dangerous' favour which he implied to me would be available on request, and encouraged George to join in the fun?

Fun: was it only that? A playful experiment with body parts? If so, would my offence be a worse one than Kit's if I let things take their course? Was the whole affair after all, of any consequence whatsoever since, to my way of thinking, love and sex had nothing much to do with each other? I had not mourned Ann's death just because I could no longer go to bed with her. Ganson had once proposed that the best physical relationships were to be enjoyed with a woman one didn't much care for, a proposition ratified by his fascination for Professor Hathaway.

These were evening thoughts, the day's anxieties pacified by a bottle of wine that, in tune with Ganson's recommendation of only drinking under lengthening shadows, occasioned a temporary reprieve, exposed the next morning as complacent and immoral. The business must be got over without further delay, coolly, calmly, mercilessly if need be. Coffee would help: and a cigarette.

CHAPTER XIII

George's attic had continued to disgorge old books. The seafaring yarn containing the incident where Sills had been sick in a bucket had been replaced by a book of non-fiction.

'Do you think our river's got tench in it?'

'I don't know. George, I want to…'

George was paying no attention. 'Listen, this is from a book called *Rod, Pole, and Perch*: "Among the pleasure meadows of that unadvertised but entrancing home of British beauty spots, Wiltshire, I have had many days fishing. It was on the Kennet and Avon canal that I caught my first and biggest tench. With a caravan drawn up in an adjacent meadow, it was a simple matter to…" What's a tench?'

'A fish.'

'You sound cross. Is that why breakfast's a bit late today?'

'I want to be serious for a moment.'

'Serious? How can you be serious when all around you are starving faces?'

'Please tell me something honestly because there is a person trying to spread nasty rumours. Is there something peculiar, sexually peculiar, going on between you and Kit?'

As soon as I'd said that, I knew it was a mistake. I was accusing George of compliance in what could only have been coercion.

George looked embarrassed. 'I suppose that man's been getting at you?'

'What man?'

'I don't know what man. A man who was spying on us and who I chased off.'

'When you say he'd been spying on you, what do you mean?'

'Well, Kit and I were sitting talking when we saw someone peering through the garden window. I thought he must be a conjuror like us, trying to find out our secrets. So I jumped up and spat, like in his face, except the glass was in the way. It was a good gob of spit with some green in it. It made the man run off. He had a funny run, like a girl's. Can I have my egg fried today, not boiled, because you do them too runny sometimes being in a hurry to get me off to…'

'When you say you and Kit were sitting talking, you were sitting on Kit's lap, were you not?'

147

'I think I may have been.'

'What were you sitting on his lap for?'

'Oh, dad, what do you think for?'

'When you sit on Kit's lap you're not fully dressed, are you?'

'I suppose the man told you that too.'

'Yes, he did, but I should have guessed it already when you came home without your Harold T-shirt which Kit divested you of. Along with everything else probably.'

'Not everything.'

'What do you mean, not everything?'

'Socks: and that. On, my socks were.'

'And he was playing around with you?'

'Well of course he was. You don't sit on someone's lap for any other reason, do you, once you're not a baby, basically. Dad, this is so embarrassing. You are meant to teach me the facts of life not the other way round.'

'Why didn't you tell me there was something wrong? Did Kit warn you it was a secret.'

'Not really. Well, no more than he warns me not to give away our conjuring secrets. I wouldn't tell my friends those.'

'Did you tell Cyrus about you and Kit?'

'I may have and I may not have.'

'You did, didn't you?

'I may have and I may not have.'

'What did he have to say about it?'

'He said it was O.K., basically. Now, can we talk about something else?'

'Why did you keep it secret from me? Did you think I was going to punish you.'

'I didn't think you'd be interested. Because, basically, you don't really know all that much about sex and stuff if you're honest with yourself. When you told me about it, you only did like the wombs and sperm bit. Anyway, why shouldn't I have a secret? You have.'

'I have not: not from you anyway.'

'Yes, you do. You have a money secret. Where do you get all that money to pay my school fees? Grandma says you have a secret stash. I bet you've got a lady hidden away, a lady you do sex with who gives you loads of money for doing It with her. That's why you're so rich.'

'That's not funny.'

'It's funny a bit.'

'It's not funny lots. We're not talking about money now, we're talking about Kit Buller. When you asked me about kippers and pigeons doing what you call It and you asked if It was not only for making babies, you were hoping I'd put your mind at rest about what Kit was making you do. Am I right?'

I could think of no other way of approaching the physicality involved without having to hear the details. It is not easy to think of one's relations having sex and if one does so it is generally to belittle them in one's eyes. What horrified me was the idea that the love Kit might feel for George as he took him upon his lap, and the love that had engulfed me the evening I had taken him upon mine (and knew then and there that he must stay with me for always and always) were of equal validity, and that in a contest such as this parenthood was powerless to affirm its natural superiority. That couldn't be. Mine was a privileged and worthy love established by law, obeyed worldwide, divinely decreed, holy, sacrosanct; and Kit was guilty of a sin forbidden by God, forbidden by man. He must be seen off before he could usurp my rightful… Here I stopped. My rightful what? Prerogative? Trophy? Goods?

'Dad, can't we just leave it?'

'We can't possibly "just leave it." I don't want my son sleeping with grown men. I don't really want my son sleeping with his own sex. It can lead to difficulties.'

'We usually stay awake.'

'That is not funny.'

'It's funny a bit.'

George awaited the corollary. I did not offer it.

'To put it another way, I don't want you having sex with someone, man or woman, three times your age and six times your size.'

'It isn't sex, not what you'd call sex. Not real sex, anyway. How can it be sex when we can't make babies?'

'Things can't continue as they are. Nor could they have continued as they were.'

'Were when?'

'Were before.'

'Before what.'

'Before I knew what I know now.'

149

'But they would have.'

'Why do you say that?'

'Because you didn't know. And now you do know and it's made it all complicated.'

'A serious crime has been committed.'

'You mean we could go to prison?'

'Kit could. Not you, of course. You are a child.'

'I am not a child.' George screamed his words. 'I am a boy; and you are a fucking retard.'

George threw over his chair, ran out of the room and out of the front door. He slammed it hard behind him.

*

I rang George's headmaster.

'Is George at school?'

'Trouble at t'mill?'

'Aye.'

'Hold on, I'll find out if he's here.'

He was in choir practice. 'Singing like an angel. Anything I can do?'

'If you could just get a message to him to leave his bicycle in the sheds after school and say that I'll pick him up in the car.'

'Will do. And why not stay for a snifter while you're at it? The decanter awaits.'

Now another theatrical interview had to be conducted. I had to face Kit with words such as 'all has been revealed.' I felt a deep repugnance that my son should be taken on to Kit's lap, stripped of his vest and of the merry pants we had bought at Caley's and in just his socks submitted to whatever fingerings his so-called friend enjoyed. Then again, what if physicality turned out to be only part and parcel of Kit's affection? Could I justifiably vent my fury on a man who loved my son? He was lovable. Was I angry only because I was jealous? Certainly not. It was repellant to think of myself forming a physical relationship with George. What I meant to say was that I was worried less about his corruption than by the fear of being parted from him either by Kit's commandeering him for his own or by the way, if I went to the police, the law might take its course and remove him from my care because, as Hathaway had implied, I had colluded in his seduction. Kit had used George only to satisfy his own needs. That was the end of the matter.

Again it crossed my mind I was using a theatrical turn of phrase. The crime though was dramatic in its enormity: in most people's eyes.

I didn't have to seek Kit out. On my way to his flat I spotted him fishing on the jetty. He was alone, seated on a stool. A wicker creel beside him recalled the basket beside the boy in his picture of the snake charmer. I walked quietly up behind him and pushed him into the river. Even before he hit the water I wondered if he could swim and if not whether I would have to rescue my son's despoiler, as Houdini's publicity agents had put it, 'from a drowning death.'

He struck out manfully and swam some distance away from the shore, breasting the water with a steady stroke as if he were enjoying a morning bathe. He turned around just as leisurely and swam back to the shore, pulling himself on to the jetty. His wet shorts revealed more than needed to be observed of the violator of my son. I shouted my accusation.

Kit smiled. 'Did I exceed the stated dose?'

From the opposite shore a boat was making towards us. It had no sail and made no sound, nor was it of any particular colour save the greyish hue of the river itself. A man in white robes stood at the prow of this craft that was slung so low in the water as to suggest her occupant glided miraculously across the river's surface. To me, to Kit too who began to wring out his shirt and stamp vigorously to release water from his clammy shorts, it seemed that whoever it was had seen the occurrence and was sailing to Kit's aid.

The occupant was Mr Welldone. He wore a shalwar-kameez of startling whiteness. He moored up but made no further move to come ashore. Far from being concerned at Kit's plight, he exhibited no surprise whatever at his soaking condition nor gave any indication that he had witnessed my assault. He called out to me:

'Good morning. How are you? We must get together soon. And tackle those Gordon letters.' He looked over my shoulder as though he might disembark and head off inland on foot, then changed his mind and re-started his whispering motor. He raised his right hand and extending his first two fingers from a closed fist pointed them skywards after the manner of a priest about to bestow a Christian blessing. Then, instead of inscribing in the air the sign of the cross, he altered the direction of his arm, turned sideways on, and aimed his two conjoined fingers horizontally as if, with a handgun, he was taking aim at an invisible enemy somewhere upstream. His thumb, that was resting on the second knuckle of his third finger as if upon the trigger of this imagined pistol, tightened inwards. His arm jerked upwards at the recoil from his firing. The message was clear: kill your enemy: shoot him dead: you've got a gun to do it with. The gun I gave you.

I turned to Kit: 'You have been messing about with my son. We'll talk about it this afternoon. I shall expect you to be at home.' I walked off.

*

Kit led me into the sitting-room where, without saying a word, he settled himself into a big armchair, the armchair most likely where he'd been overlooked with George on his knee. He spread his arms wide, a signal that he was open to some sort of a discussion. In a minute, when I produced Mr Welldone's weapon, he'd be raising them above his head. I brought it out swiftly from my righthand jacket pocket. In my confusion about how to proceed with a cross-examination no less impossible to conduct with any coherence than the breakfast interview with George, I found I was holding it the wrong way round. I thought to hit him over the head with what in my hand was now only a blunt instrument and instead overturned the silver-framed picture of his mythical girl friend on the table by his chair and brought the butt hard down on it, smashing the glass. Only then did I point the barrel at Kit's heart. He stared it unflinchingly down.

'You never believed she was my fiancée, did you? I could tell from your face. I found her in a magazine. She looked the kind of woman a man, a real man you'd probably say, ought to have around.'

Even discounting Kit's training in an elite military regiment, where he would surely have been taught how to defend himself against an armed opponent, how many men, I wondered, had been relieved of their weapon by an untrained victim simply knocking it out of their hands and telling them not to make an ass of themselves? And how many of those antagonists had no intention of pulling the trigger in a confrontation that, with a man lying dead, would have laid them open to a life in gaol? From the beginning I felt as little sense of security at being armed as my enemy showed insecurity at my armament. Kit may have reckoned that I had no intention of killing him for the very good reason that I would be imprisoned for murder and parted for ever

152

from the son I had avenged: yet he gave no sign of what in his mind, regardless of his army training, must have been an uncertainty, whether or not the father before him would be desperate enough to pull the trigger, or whether an apology for his actions if pathetically enough delivered, might merit some stay of justice. He neither begged for mercy nor made any move to unarm me. Instead, he set up a fighting front, unburdening himself of various excuses for his behaviour to which he added a flippancy of tone that may have been prompted by nervousness that he was after all facing death and that, before he succumbed, he needed to inform me of his weakness and instill in me, after I'd shot him dead, a sense of misgiving for his murder.

'Our lot is a reviled race. For we are a race, you know. We are everywhere. You'll never be rid of us. We are men, but men not grown sexually to maturity, so we do not require mature gratification. Neither does a boy. So where's the harm? You're labouring under the apprehension that boys who go with men develop similar tendencies as if they had been in contact with an infectious disease. Complete bollocks. I am not carrying germs and even if I were George's immune system would reject them.'

'That is the apologia of a perverted man. Yours is a sin forbidden by God, an outrage condemned by man. I cannot for a moment condone your actions.'

This was parodic, the splutterings of a retired officer of militia with a white moustache bristling at an affront, curiously akin to Major Scott's fulmination when in my schooldays he had rounded on me for my interest in spiritualism.

'You mean you can't be seen to condone them. Parents can't, you understand, because we offer an extension of parental love, a love inclusive of sex, a sin indeed in a boy's father, a sin forbidden by God, an outrage condemned by man, as you rightly observe, a far more unpardonable sin, I think you would agree, than this indiscretion of my own.'

'What has George gained from your attentions?'

'He is a better conjuror.'

'He has certainly become a master of deception.'

'He has never deceived you. He has merely kept his mouth shut.'

'At your request, most probably. At your urgent bidding, fearing yet another spell inside. If you must sleep with your own sex, why not choose someone of your own age?'

'Why would I want to sleep with someone who looks like me when I'm in bed with him every night of my life? Isn't the point of sex the pleasure experienced by the juxtaposition of opposites?'

Kit made as if to stand up. I altered the aim of the pistol. He sat back again.

'I am not here to discuss sexual ethics.'

'So be it.' Kit shrugged his shoulders.

This impasse could not continue if I were not to suggest, by upholding the silence that had fallen across the room, a concordance, Kit might even venture a sympathy, with the psychological make-up of men such as he. Born, I later saw, out of a determination to bring him to justice, and at the same time to get out of his house without prolonging a deadlocked confrontation, I came up with the perfect *coup de grâce*.

'We none of us, you, me, George, can go about our lives in the same way as before. There is only one possible solution. You know what you must do.' I handed him the gun. I turned my back on him and walked out of the room.

I made my way along the verandah, past the kitchen where the boy in the lithograph, 'Try My Soup', laughed in my face. '"Shag My Bum" more like,' Aldhouse had said during an exegesis on the Newlyn school of art from whose ranks he had chosen Stanhope Forbes over Henry Scott Tuke whose broadly grinning model he did not appreciate. 'I've never seen such a little tart. Tuke was boy-mad of course. In my opinion boys in paintings should be observed from a distance: like cows.'

Only later did I wonder why Kit had not put a bullet in the back of my head.

I met George in the car at his school gates. He jumped in beside me and put his arms around me.

'I love you, dad. And you're not a retard.'

'I am a retard a bit.'

'You're not a retard lots.'

'I love you more than anyone else in the world. In fact you are the only person in the world I love so you can have all I have to offer and that's a whacking amount.'

'And you're not going to send me back to grandma?'

'Why ever should I do that?'

'As a punishment.'

'But you've done nothing wrong. It's Kit who's misbehaved himself.'

154

'And do you think I could go on seeing him if I asked him not to do the cuddling stuff?'

'We'll see.'

Here was a phrase I had heard Molly use in reply to a request from her grandson. As a rule of thumb, George could reckon the odds that his wishes would be granted stood at sixty to forty, give or take. The future would take care of that, if future there were to be of the kind of life we'd enjoyed in the past. What if Kit shot himself, though? How could it be kept from George to whom of course I would say nothing about my two encounters with him after our breakfast contretemps that I had driven his friend to despair and death? In that dreadful event, a good plan would be to plant in George's mind the suggestion that Kit had been assassinated in the course of SAS duties he had briefly taken up again in a secret military emergency.

He wouldn't kill himself, of course. He'd shown himself too tough for that. Nevertheless, what an ass I had made of myself. Of all the posturings I had adopted, the outrage of a father, his threat of physical violence, of informing the police, the specious advice given to his son, his expostulation at Kit's admission of his failings, his noisy disgust at perversion and his bungled assassination of the man who had ruined a young life, the one that was the most futile and the most melodramatic had been the one on which he had acted.

Again and again, the fear returned that Kit would do what I had ordered him to do. Unable to face another prison sentence, he might choose to take his own life. Then I could be jailed as an accessory before the fact and George taken into care. Our happy life together was in jeopardy if the truth were ever to come out. Surely, though, Kit would not act on my command. He'd accept it for what it was, a novelistic, half-witted, melodramatic riposte by a parent who refused to look clinically at a domestic crisis. He'd just up sticks and move on. That was a comfort.

Comparative calm was short-lived. On the doormat was a letter from Kit:

Dear Leonard:

When I was in the SAS we were issued with a small capsule, to be taken before carrying out the sort of especially dangerous mission that those commanding us thought we would be too chicken to perform without

155

an artificial stimulant. Each man was given one single pill, to be returned when he retired or was transferred from the Service. In my rather hurried expulsion, which I suppose you have learned about by now from that trespassing old bitch, they forgot to ask me for it back. I thought of taking it before my court appearance but resisted doing so, worrying perhaps that it was not a pill to boost courage but a suicide capsule (we never knew with our bosses quite how far they'd go to serve their own ends).

I have now taken it and am amazed by its stimulation. I am certain I shall be able to perform the task you set me with a clear head. As well as courage, whatever chemical the capsule possesses donates an unexpected clarity of vision and under its influence I am going to set out something of my nature, I mean our nature, for there is a whole nation of us as I told you, a reviled one, although you do not see it that way. Then I'll get on with the job you've set me.

We have no desire to copy the ways of normal men, you would say. Coupling is for couples. In our game, one should request, never command. Most of the time all one can hope for is an indifference to an advance when there might have been rejection. Never offer drugs or drink as an inducement. Boys are lousy lovers at the best of times. Cannabis and vodka slammers put the kibosh on the whole enterprise. Besides poisoning them, it makes them feel grown-up which is of course the last thing we want them to be. Cigarettes used to be permissible although there is a risk these days that parents will smell the tobacco. Despite your habit, George is a dyed-in-the-wool non-smoker. That's why he asked me how to make cigarettes magically disappear. (By the way, he needs a new elastic for that pull). Of course our lot is rapacious, though I prefer to say, acquisitive. How can we not be constantly on the search for a soul-mate when our soul-mate has a life expectancy of five years at the most before he begins to resemble ourselves?

The professor and her kind have made a lucrative cottage industry out of our indiscretions. They consign us to long prison sentences and take money for our treatment inside and, because they have made the world believe that an incurable harm has been done to our 'victims,' they batten themselves onto their parents and make still more money by convincing them what a mess their offspring will turn out to be without their expertise. The papers are full of stories of tiresome old shags recalling how they had their bottoms pinched in the year dot and how their lives would have been ruined for ever after had it not been for psychotherapy.

Truth to tell, I was surprised when George condescended. Georges are on my list of non-goers. Certain names set my pulses racing, others are on my list of non-goers. George is one of the latter. Along with Ruperts, Leonards (no wonder you are so hostile), Mileses, Gileses, Rowlands (with or without the w), Barneys – God protect us from Barneys – Bens, Henrys ... The best name, I hear you ask? Stephen, unquestionably; but it must be with a 'ph.'

Nuff said.

Your last words to me were, 'You know what you must do.'

I do indeed.

Kit.

P.S. What an interesting weapon you have given me for the job. It is of Hungarian make. We had an example at SAS HQ. How on earth did you come by it?

CHAPTER XIV

On the morning of the funeral, rain, diluvial in quantity, coursing from fat-bellied clouds of Stygian darkness lumbering from the west over mist-enshrouded hills, heralded a thunderstorm of apocalyptic proportions as if the reprisals I anticipated later in the day from the world of men had been pre-empted by chthonian entities. George was also in stormy mood although his was the miasmic torpor of a plague of locusts rather than the racket going on overhead. He was chromatically arrayed in a fleecy garment which, together with a selection of other clothes, had been received from Oo May Fashions. A cheque had been enclosed in the parcel together with a letter addressed to me that read in part:

At this moment in time, it is our hope that there may no longer exist any further issues between us. To further this end, please find enclosed a goodwill payment in the sum of one hundred pounds. We also send herewith a selection of goods from our Kids' Wearing Experience KWEX© range that we hope will prove acceptable. May we express the hope that you may find yourself to be of the same conciliatory frame of mind?

The car wouldn't start. George reckoned it had been struck by a bolt of lightning which had blown its electrical system. He had been asked to swell the numbers of the church choir, the village organist having heard something of his school prowess in that direction. One minute he'd said he'd go, the next that he'd no intention of singing at an observance that would make him miserable, finally running after me at the last moment. The rain followed us on our walk until our arrival at the church coincided with a clearing sky. On the horizon another storm was gathering. Lightning flashed over by the river. These sudden fluctuations of torrential rain, blazing sun, black clouds, blue sky, presaged the events with which the day would be as violently punctuated as the claps of thunder and the blinding rays of sunshine piercing the bruised clouds, which threatened an even heavier downpour than the one that had abated. For my part, arrival at the church in good time for the service had no more been a plan than to attend the funeral at all. My presence might be construed as the glee of the assassin as he watches his victim's coffin lowered into the earth, knowing that he has achieved his aim. I recalled an adage of Yseult Pash's:

> 'In whichever temple you find yourself,
> honour the Gods therein.'

In obedience to her admonition, I would, in this church, offer thanks to her God for the disentanglement from a person who threatened our lives, mine and my son's.

Ganson stepped out from behind a tombstone where he had been pulling on a cigarette.

'Give me that,' George said.

'Say please.'

'Please.'

'You're rather young to be smoking, aren't you?'

'I'm not going to smoke it. I strongly disapprove of smoking as my father will tell you and as I shall now demonstrate to the astonishment of all present.'

Ganson handed him his lighted cigarette which George thrust into his closed fist. He performed a deft vanish.

'Shiver my timbers, how does he do that?'

George walked off.

'This is a shocking business,' Ganson said. 'Imagine being discovered dead on the lav. Bad enough being discovered alive on it.'

A man came hurrying out of the vestry door.

'Mr Ganson?'

'Yes.'

'Thought it was. I remember making you chuckle at Sir Guy Wendon's wedding with one of my famous yarns. We must all get together for another chinwag one day in the near future. But now, to business. I've got a man in the vestry sheltering from the rain. Says his name is Scott.'

I recognized Hawley Fawcett.

Ganson had not forgotten his hostility to Fawcett at the marriage feast. 'If he says his name is Scott, the chances are it very probably is. Ask him to come out and join us in a fag.'

'He's in a wheelchair.'

'What on earth has the idiot done now?' Ganson turned to me. 'What do you make of this? Bloody Scottie McLeod, fallen down another ski slope I suppose, or broken a leg in a rugby scrum. *Je te demande*. What the hell's he doing here anyway?'

159

'He may be putting in some fieldwork on the more dolorous ceremonies of the Anglican church in preparation for a class on the burial rites of all nations.'

'I suppose he might. Very well, I'll come and push him along but I'll give him a piece of my mind while I'm about it. I hope to God he's fit enough for Tuesday's seminars. You'll want to stay here and get Mr Fawcett to run over that comical story again in case you missed a nuance or two first time round. Wait for me here at the end of the service and I'll give you and that bugger McLeod a lift. And his fucking wheelchair. It looks like rain again.' He made off. Hawley too was not disposed to hang around.

'I must cut along as well, more's the pity,' he said. 'It's all go here today. We've got a christening later on.'

The church was almost empty. A smell of incense from an earlier ceremony lingered in the air. It was pleasantly warm, unusually so for churches, often left unheated by their incumbents to point up the austerity of the Christian faith. The few in attendance had seated themselves well apart from each other. None of them was familiar. The organ wheezed solemn notes. I chose a pew to the side. The wall on my left displayed a series of framed watercolours illustrating Bible scenes, 'The Woman of Canaan,' 'The Pool of Bethesda,' (a man on crutches on the bath's edge recalled Scottie after one of his sporting mishaps), 'Christ Walking on the Water', 'Palm Sunday,' the scribe addressing Jesus as 'Master.' Their serrated edges and Gothic captions proposed them to be the original drawings for stamps designed long ago to be stuck in bibles by Sunday School children as proof of their attendance. The disarming execution of these overly bright scenes reflected the simple faith of those who regularly worshipped here. I was alone in the pew. Thoughts trailed distractedly. The conclusion seemed to be that things were back to normal, violently though this condition had been achieved. If normal, they could be called. And then only for the time being. It had to be faced that, by some devious route, I could be associated with the ownership of the gun that killed the deceased, an accessory before the fact, therefore. Its donor, Mr Welldone, who seemed to know everything about everyone, could put two and two together and, to test the truth of his theory, ask me for the return of his weapon. I wondered what had become of it.

The rector took his place at the pulpit. He bade us stand for a hymn.

'Let us sing together "The day Thou gavest Lord is ended."'

The congregation sang only feebly. It was as well that the choir was in attendance in the organ loft behind me. The day appeared ended indeed, as another storm darkened the church's windows. Over the rolls of thunder, the rector intoned: 'Almighty God, with whom do live the spirits of them that depart hence in the Lord, and with whom the souls of the faithful, after they are delivered from the burden of the flesh, are in joy and felicity; we give thee hearty thanks, for that it hath pleased thee to deliver this our brother from the miseries of this sinful world; beseeching thee...'

The rector paused. He had made a fearful mistake. He may have been unnerved by a degree of hostility among those present at his being assigned the task of burying this person simply because he was the incumbent of the deceased's parish when the congregation might have preferred the service to be conducted by a priest of its own choice: or secularly at the crematorium to which the body was later to be consigned. Someone coughed. A hymn book fell or had been thrown in anger to the floor. The rector had no choice but to re-intone the passage from the beginning.

'Almighty God, with whom do live the spirits of them that depart hence in the Lord, and with whom the souls of the faithful, after they are delivered from the burden of the flesh, are in joy and felicity; we give thee hearty thanks, for that it hath pleased thee to deliver this our sister from the miseries of this sinful world; beseeching thee...'

Centrally placed on the altar steps, the coffin rested on its trestles. It resembled a stage property into which a magician would hand a smiling woman prior to her being sawn in half. Kit Buller had commented on these mutilations: 'Best thing that could happen to them.' Well, he had got his wish, that was for sure, exacted a terrible revenge not only by murdering the woman about to denounce him to the authorities but by ensuring her end had about it nothing of grace. Kit had chosen to interpret my departing words to him, 'you know what you must do,' as an order to dispose of a person who was getting in the way, mine as well as his, the implication was, of a pattern of life he had no intention of giving up.

I wondered if he had fired the shot or, with the use of one of the SAS's powerful drugs, persuaded Professor Hathaway to shoot herself and then orchestrated the demeaning tableau 'with clothing disarranged' –

the phrase she had used to describe her killer's embraces with my son – so that it looked like suicide.

The clergyman broke off his invocations, bade us sit down, and said some informal words. There was a brief hiatus as he beckoned a man from the sparsely occupied pews. He ascended the pulpit vacated by the officiant and after polishing and placing on his nose a pair of spectacles covering only the lower half of his eyes, tried unavailingly to launch into what would most likely be some kind of encomium.

He cleared his throat of a bubble of phlegm or choked back prevailing tears. He gave his name and credentials.

'Being descended from England's greatest poet, it should come as no surprise that Mona Rosamund Hathaway wrote poetry herself. I'd like to commence my memorial by reading a few of her lines:

> How all things transitory, all things vain
> Desert me! Whither am I sinking slow
> On the prone wing, to what predestined home,
> What peace beyond all peace, what ultimate joy?
> Nay, cease from questioning, care not to know,
> Let bliss dissolve each thought, all function cease,
> Fold close the wing, let the soft-flowing light
> Permeate, and merely once uplift drooped lids
> To mark the world remote, the abandoned shore,
> Fretted with much vain pleasure, futile pain,
> Far, far.

Not bad. Not bad at all. But not by the dead woman, Rosamund Hathaway or whatever her real name was, one, according to Ganson, to invoke visions of the washing-up. The lines were by Edward Dowden, a poet I had briefly considered as my candidate for Ganson's Sunk Without Trace project. Dowden was little enough known for the woman to hijack one of his poems and pass it off as her own. It was enterprising of her to have dug so deeply into my world of minor poetry but then she had been a vastly enterprising woman. Enterprising enough to have commandeered my son and made him a shield behind which she could wage her dreary battle over the Oo May trademark.

The speaker went on: '... then for a while she wrote for the local paper for this area. People will remember Roz's "Happy to Help" column that ran for some time while she was pursuing her studies for a higher degree in social psychology which she eventually passed with flying colours, being awarded a professorship by the International Philotechnical University of West Hartlepool. By then, she had married the prosperous shipping magnate, Akilles Abecassis, but she soon concluded wedded life was not for her because it interfered with her vital youth work in the community. Her trenchant understanding of kids' welfare stood her in good stead on a commercial as well as a counselling level, although of course her caring ways always came before the financial consideration she received when she was recruited by the consultancy division of the celebrated fashion house, Oo May, to meaningfully interact with their juvenile clients.'

Now, the man's testimonial took an extraordinary turn: 'We can never know but we may suppose it was her selflessness and her concern for others that forbore this fragrant lady's consideration to how weakly were her own defences. We cannot be sure, such are the ways of big business, if her sudden dismissal from the clothing chain for which she had selflessly worked affected her health and, since no representative is present today, we may not be too harsh in finding them partially guilty for her being taken from us. There again, that may be unfair. Roz had a heart of gold, but gold, my friends, is a precious metal, envied by all, a temptation to thieves. It was Roz's heart of gold that was snatched from her before her time, purloined like a valuable ring and a sudden heart attack took from us our vibrant companion.'

The speaker paused to allow his metaphor its deserved plaudits. I would gladly have risen in assent. Rosamund Scrubbs had died a natural death. Dead of a heart attack, not done to death, not murdered, not shot by a bullet from the weapon supplied to her killer by a victim of her extortions. Dead of a heart attack. Death 'due to natural causes.' A wonder had occurred, an event as miraculous as any of the biblical scenes on the wall at my side.

Unless, of course, Kit had administered the mortal SAS pill he had mentioned might be in his possession. No, that couldn't be. His letter said he'd only got one pill which he had taken and which had given him the courage to act on my request. 'You know what you must do?' 'I do indeed' he had written in what I had assumed to be his suicide note, whereas in fact he'd taken no action at all and was even now among the choir in the organ-loft. So, either he intended to shelve the whole affair or whatever plan he had in in mind lay in the future. So far as I was concerned, I, as the accessory to Hathaway's death, was in the clear. That was the main thing.

To whom should I give thanks for this deliverance? To the God in whose temple I found myself of course. When next we were bidden to kneel, I would offer up my praise for His sudden destruction of a malevolent and dirty-minded woman. Yet, as I steadied myself against the joyful emotions bursting from me, I needed to consider earthly matters which were yet to be resolved.

For a reason that became disturbingly apparent, my thoughts returned to Edward Dowden whose poem the dead woman had passed off as her own. I reflected why, of all Goethe's poetry, he had chosen to translate the *West-East Divan*. German speakers had complained of his rendering *Schenke* as 'tavern' in the lines:

> Yes, in the tavern I too have been seated.
> For me, as for the rest, the wine was meted.

Goethe's seemingly throwaway lines reporting how he had once sat drinking at his ease in some place of refreshment or other revealed his knowledge of a surreptitious commerce available within this establishment other than the open consumption of wine. I could answer with Goethe that I too, in my early days, frequented an illicit tavern although I had been not the drinker there but the cup-bearer, performing a service to which, according to our academy's German professor, Dr Muller, Goethe had been sympathetic. 'I wasn't aware it was that sort of a bar' he had remarked of the place where we had met and, as he said those words, had waved an effeminate hand. Here was something I had dismissed from my mind as unnecessary to consider in the course of the dire business fetching up in this church. My boyhood stint in Goethe's figurative 'divan' could be ignored no longer. In a way it had fashioned my whole life. I, as a cup-bearer, had meted wine to the man who had financed, still did finance, my existence, mine and George's, the man too who had rescued me from occult practices. To him, as Amos had said when he showed me his scarred face, I needed to be eternally grateful.

Cup-bearers, if consulted, would most likely say they would prefer not to have to bear cups, there being plenty of other things they'd rather do, play computer games, kick a football, make model aircraft, climb rocks, go swimming, in my case call up the dead on school Sundays.

It had to be conceded, though, it is a position not without rewards, a position that, as life goes on, one comes to see played a vital part in fashioning one's future.

The orator had reached his end. The clergyman asked the congregation to stand. The organ began again, on a happier level this time, suggestive of the riddance of a contemptible woman from the land of the living. The choir struck up 'For All the Saints' into whose company, despite the burden of the hymn, Rosamund Hathaway would be hard pressed to find a place.

From outside where the sun had come out again, a ray of light fell upon one of the series of the New Testament pastels displayed on the wall to my left. 'Christ Walking on the Water' revived memories of Mr Welldone when he had appeared in his motor-boat after I had pushed Kit into the river. Yseult Pash had addressed him as 'Master,' or so George had said. The scribe in the neighbouring pastel was addressing Christ as Master, the 'mastering me God' to whom Hopkins, not a favourite of mine, had also appealed. I had taken Yseult's 'Masters' to be nothing but fictitious know-alls. She had insisted they were real people, further, that they had supernatural powers. This seemed not entirely out of the question considering Mr Welldone, or Count Racokzy, had promised, when he learned George and I were related, that he would look after us in the same way as he was apparently keeping an eye on Auntie Salt. His disappearance after he had planted his gun on me seemed to have been part of his plan. Now that he had set everyone back on their path there would be no further need for communication. In my newfound euphoria of gratitude to whichever god – or master – had brought events to this pass I was prepared to believe Yseult was right: that the Count, calling upon his miraculous endowments, had delivered me and my son from the clutches of a fiend.

'And now, to God the Father, God the Son and God the Holy Ghost be all honour and glory now and for ever more. World without end. Amen.'

The choir echoed the spoken doxology. 'Worms without heads are men.' George might have intoned this variant he had learned in the school singing classes, amusing Kit who was by his side. The coffin was paraded down the central aisle. The congregation slowly followed.

I sat on until the church had emptied out and made my way to the door. Outside rain now steadily fell. Neither Ganson nor Scottie was among the small group huddled under umbrellas. Ganson had probably forgotten he was to pick me up or, more likely, had decided to dodge the funeral altogether. Scottie and he were probably in a pub somewhere by now. I decided to return to the warmth of the church's interior until the weather brightened up again. The heavy door swung back on well-oiled hinges, emitting a burst of warmth. The interior was more brightly lit than it had been for the funeral as if extra illumination had been switched on to display a stage setting arranged in my absence and prepared as a fascination for my eyes alone. Two figures in cassock and surplice knelt before the altar. Their bent heads, one golden, one dark, were composed in a scene of devotion, the honest Christian devotion that had been impressed on me by the biblical paintings on the church wall. George and Kit Buller were at prayer.

I had an idea of joining them in their prayers and in thanksgiving to the god in the temple wherein I found myself for interceding on my behalf. Were I to do so, I would ask the two of them to move apart and kneel between my son and Kit in emphasis of the difference, as George had put it, between love and love and love and It.

The illusion didn't last long. Kit and George were not praying. There was a rattle of money. Some loose change had escaped their fingers. The coins rolled rattling down the altar steps. George got up, hurried after them, retrieved them, ran back again, fell once more to his knees. Metal clinked again on metal. Kit and George were performing coin tricks.

The uplifting concepts that, a moment go, had been evoked by the kneeling couple, exemplifying further than had already been established in my mind the sanctity of the temple on whose threshold I stood and the inherent virtuousness of the two worshippers, were now as precipitately dashed by the irreverence, if not blasphemy, of these two fraudulent miracle-workers' pretension to superhuman powers. I brought to mind my school-friend Amos, the self-appointed magus of our spiritualistic séances. A vision of his fearfully scarred face floated before my eyes, the disfigured face of a man, or perhaps Amos had still been a boy when the horror was visited upon him, on whom had descended the wrath of the God he had impertinently mimicked in his invocation of demonic spirits. That was his punishment for muddling with magic, magic that was only one step away from the parlour tricks in progress in this holy place. My fears that George might

166

follow in Amos's footsteps, those fears that had been allayed by Kit – 'he's a sensible fellow' he had assured me – possessed me once more. I was about to march up the aisle and order George out of the church when my way was stopped.

I heard Ganson's voice behind me. 'I must leave this gentleman in your care. Otherwise I'll be late for the seminar and then where would we be? Pressures, pressures...' Before I could turn round and sympathise or remonstrate with McLeod for yet another example of his recklessness in the sporting arena, a hand grabbed my arm as if its owner, who I knew immediately was not our colleague's, urgently sought my aid. A ring on one of the fingers of that restraining hand burned into my wrist as if the flesh had been submitted to a branding iron. As the grip tightened ever more firmly, the heat altered to an intense cold and from an ancient memory that, however agitated I felt when quite often these identical fingers had stayed my hand, it would have been discourteous, not to say impolitic, to shake off the restraint.

'Leonard Saunders.'

'He says his name is Scott.' That was the name Hawley, the verger, had given for the man he had in his care. Both Ganson and I assumed he referred to our religious studies lecturer, Scottie McLeod, confined to a wheelchair on account of some sporting injury.

'So we meet yet again.' Major Scott looked up from his chair and shyly smiled. 'Don't look so surprised. I know we're meant to be attending a funeral and not a resurrection from the tomb. The fact of the matter is, though, Rosamund Scrubbs, "Nosy Posy" I always called her, was my wife's daughter. Well, I say my wife, but she wasn't of course, as you probably guessed ages ago.'

'It never crossed my mind.'

Major Scott chuckled: tittered, rather, putting a hand to his mouth to cover the unambiguously false teeth that had replaced the protrusions of his younger days. He seemed to have grown slightly effeminate in his old age.

'Come, come, Leonard, your old gentleman friend, married? Not bloody likely. You must have been aware I was not the marrying kind. She was a gold-digger, was dear old April Scrubbs, but useful to me in hooking me up to young companions. I had to reward her for that of course, pay her hotel bills, that sort of thing. And her pansy masseur. What was the name of the old shack we lived in?'

167

'The Irving.'

'That's it. April was very annoyed that I clung on to you for so long. She earned not a penny from me for three years. Tell me while we have a moment, were you upset when I threw you over? I didn't have time to ask you that when we met in the care home.'

It would have been cruel to tell Major Scott that after the initial bewilderment I was almost entirely unmoved at our parting except for the loss of my five-pound bus-fares and that I'd only kept him sweet for such a long time because I wanted him to teach me to drive.

'I got over it.'

'I'm glad. You see, so far as I was concerned, you died when you became sixteen and it was only fair I should be dead to you too. "I had attached one young friend to me, the better friend for being young; but that's over" as Dickens wrote.'

At this point Kit and George rose from their knees and turned round. At each end of the stone-flagged passage, a new tableau resolved itself as the two sets of differentially aged companions faced each other, I with my ancient driving instructor: my son and his instructor in the magic arts. The two cup-bearers, the two frequenters of Goethe's diwan, locked eyes. No-one spoke. We were too far away from each other for speech. To call out would be to break the silence of the church, a holy silence, it could be said, undisturbed by the goings-on at the altar rails. A mute signal of recognition at last came from George who raised one side of his cassock above his ankle to reveal his right foot. He mouthed the words, 'Sensible shoes.'

I gave him a thumbs-up sign, a light-hearted acknowledgement of the long-standing feud between father and son concerning formal footwear. The gesture was intercepted by Kit. He too gave a thumbs-up. He must have taken my gesture as one of connivance in a job well done or as an intimation that all was now well between us. Major Scott took my wrist again. Once again, I left my hand where it was.

'The boy is your son, isn't he?'

'How do you know that?'

'Leonard, dear, dear, Leonard, he has the same tilt of the head as you had when you were concentrating on your driving. And the man, who is he?'

'A friend.'

'A special friend?'

'How do you know that?'

'Leonard, dear, dear Leonard…'

'Yes.'

'Does it worry you?'

'Yes.'

'It shouldn't. It didn't, did it.'

'No.'

'It won't last. It didn't, did it.'

'No.'

'Ready for the off, Mr Stocks? Your ambulance is here.' Hawley Fawcett, now in his black verger's gown, made to wheel the Major away. 'I'm sorry to have to chivvy you good people but the christening party's arriving any moment and it would be better if the two groups didn't clash if you catch my meaning. What with one party celebrating a death, well not celebrating, marking more like, and the other a birth as it were, it could easily upset the applecart. Weather's clearing up. We're in for a fine day from now on, mark my words. That comical friend of yours,' he said to me, 'asked me to tell you he'll be in the pub if required.'

'Goodbye once more,' Major Scott held out his hand 'Remember what I said.'

By now George had joined us. He watched Major Scott being wheeled away. 'Who's the old man?'

'Professor Hathaway's step-father. Sort of.'

'Kit and me agree all that singing's made us hungry. He said he'd buy me fish and chips. You too if you want to come.'

'No. Yes.'

'Cool. He was worried you might not want to. Dad, I've got a really important question to ask you. Me and Kit have been quarrelling a bit about it. He said you were the only person who could put us on the right road.'

'I'm not sure I know the answer.'

'I haven't asked you the question yet.'

'You'd better ask it, then.'

'What's the plural of "daddy-longlegs"?'

Also Published by Applecourt Books
email - camerajournal@hotmail.com

The Unpardonable Crime of Poverty.
The Letters of Frederick Rolfe to George MaQuay. Edited with an Introduction by Robert Scoble.
Baron Corvo was in such financial difficulty in early 1903 that he sought a buyer for his original genealogical wall chart of the Borgia family. Among those to whom he offered his *Borgiada* was the philanthropist William Waldorf Astor. Astor's private secretary, George Maquay, sent him a formal rejection of this offer, but later wrote a private letter expressing his admiration for Rolfe's book *Chronicles of the House of Borgia*. Sensing that he may have found a sympathetic patron, Rolfe inaugurated a sequence of lively letters which reveal interesting details about his life and writing, including his plans for two sequels to his remarkable novel *Hadrian the Seventh*. Maquay's replies have been lost. Rolfe's side of this correspondence is published here for the first time. Limited edition of 100 numbered copies

Talking About Ken Russell by Paul Sutton.
Hundreds of exclusive interviews with Ken Russell and his colleagues including, for example, fourteen cast and crew members of *Women in Love* and twenty-three first hand testimonies from *The Devils*. This landmark book provides a compelling portrait of the man and his art from his photography career in the 1950s to the great films he made in the 1960s and 1970s, and from the cult films of the 1980s to his own Viking Funeral.
978-0993177040

Into the Dark by Nicholas Wilde. The internationally acclaimed novel that was adapted into a 3-part BBC radio play and will soon become a major film. A boy on holiday at the Norfolk Coast befriends a boy his own age and is drawn towards a repeat of a double tragedy that happened a hundred years ago. A haunting story with a richly poetic climax. Nicholas Wilde, a master of the English ghost story, deftly combines a supernatural theme with a sensitive understanding of young emotions as he explores the joys and the hurts of friendship, the reaching out, and the letting go.
978-1916884601

Down Came a Blackbird by Nicholas Wilde. Nominated for the Carnegie Medal. Nicholas Wilde's third novel probes deeply into the mind of an unloved boy, whose nightmares fuse with the lost dreams of those who lived in an old dark house long before he was born. This deeply moving and quietly chilling novel was filmed as **The Ghost of Greville Lodge**, starring George Cole and Prunella Scales.

978-1916884649

To Each His Own Dolce Vita: in the Golden Age of Italian Cinema 1948-1972 by John Francis Lane. Lane came of age in an England facing decades of post-war austerity and food rationing, and where a man could be ruined and imprisoned for the crime of being born gay. Unable to resist a man in uniform, he decided to live first in Paris, where he studied filmmaking at the IDHEC. Seeing Vittorio De Sica's *The Bicycle Thieves* convinced him that the most interesting cinema was being made in Italy. He moved to Rome where he befriended De Sica and Federico Fellini, Michelangelo Antonioni, Francesco Rosi and Pier Paolo Pasolini. He appears on screen in many of their most famous films, including the defining masterpieces of the era, *L'Avventura* and *La Dolce Vita*, for which he also supervised the English-language version. He's the monk being led to Hell by the boy angel in Pasolini's *The Canterbury Tales*. He has an important role in Dino Risi's cult film, *Il Sorpasso*. Fellini's *Roma* ends with John Francis Lane and Gore Vidal toasting the end of the world. This new edition of Lane's memoirs adds more than a third of a million words, restores dozens of adventures, and includes references to more than a thousand films as he observes from the inside the rise and fall of the Golden Age of Italian Cinema.   978-1999723187

Falling Upwards: Scenes from a Life. Tim Dry's memoir of a life in arts, rises and falls through the worlds of art school, mime and pop, where he tours with Gary Numan and makes a high-wire appearance on stage with Duran Duran. He plays monsters in *Return of the Jedi* and *Xtro*, makes a globetrottery of expensive commercials, works with Joan Collins, Rutger Hauer and Mick Jagger, presents a food programme on Channel 4, and experiments with drugs to channel the ghost of Baudelaire as he begins a literary career.   978-1999723163

Paul Dufficey, The Art of Collage with a foreword by Terry Gilliam.
First Edition of 50 copies signed by Paul Dufficey.
Available exclusively from camerajournal@hotmail.com

Paul Dufficey was discovered by Derek Jarman who saw two of his paintings in the Young Contemporaries exhibition in London in 1971 and hired him to create drawings, paintings and sculpture for *Savage Messiah*, Ken Russell's film about Henri Gaudier-Brzeska. As a result, Dufficey got the nod to design all the sets, props and graphics for Ken Russell's Pop Art masterpiece, *Tommy* (1975). He also designed Russell's film *Aria* and the opera *Il Mefistofele*, which caused a riot in Genoa. In addition to his collages and his work in the cinema and the opera house, this first ever book about Paul Dufficey showcases his oil paintings, his book illustrations, new digital paintings and the great Brueghel Ceiling at Kentwell Hall in Suffolk, where he also painted the massive Shakespearean frieze on the theme of The Spirit of England.

INTO THE DARK
Nicholas Wilde

"Rich in suspense and atmosphere" — The Guardian

Down Came a Blackbird
Nicholas Wilde

"A taut and spook-filled, chillingly accurate about teenage alienation." — The Guardian

THE UNPARDONABLE CRIME OF POVERTY

The Letters of Frederick Rolfe to George Maquay

Edited with an Introduction by ROBERT SCOBLE

TALKING ABOUT
KEN RUSSELL
PAUL SUTTON

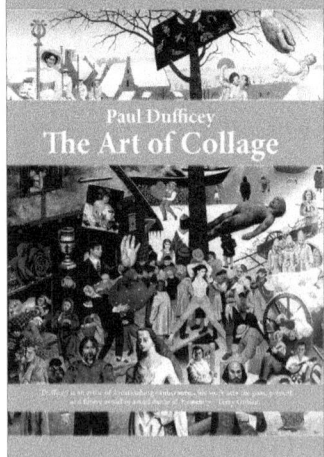

Paul Dufficey
The Art of Collage

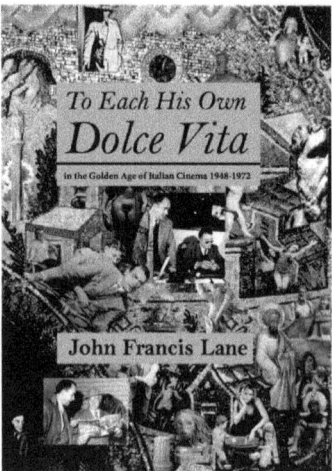

To Each His Own
Dolce Vita
in the Golden Age of Italian Cinema 1948-1972

John Francis Lane

camerajournal@hotmail.com